STAY

A Blackcreek Novel

By: Riley Hart

Edited by Making Manuscripts

Cover photo: "wings of desire"
by jackson photografix

Dedication:

To the Riley's Rebels Facebook group. Thanks for all the support, conversation, and good times. You guys are the best.

Chapter One

One after one, Braden Roth watched as people trickled out of Wes's sister's home.

He hadn't seen Wes in a while, which didn't really surprise him. Wes avoided him as much as he could ever since the one and only night they spent together. The night Wes snuck out on him while Braden slept.

Still, he continued to linger, hoping for a minute alone with Wes.

Which was a fucked-up hope in itself. Why did it bother him so much that Wes wanted nothing to do with him?

"You sticking around?" Cooper, his buddy from the firehouse, stepped up beside him, his arm in a sling from a fire he'd gotten injured in.

"Yeah, I figure so. He might need some help or something."

Coop shook his head. "He has his other sister here for that. Do you really think it's a good idea to hit on the man the day he buried his sister?"

Braden clenched his jaw, fighting not to grind his teeth the way he used to as a kid. "No shit, man. I just…" *Think he needs a friend… He looks lonely…*

"Can you blame me for asking? You have to admit, you've been relentless in trying to get him into bed again."

"That was before I knew the whole story. I'm not a total asshole, Coop." Even though he really was one. The truth was, Braden had never had a man *or* a woman sneak out on him after sex. Even if he hadn't sensed something different about Wes, that fact alone made him curious. Maybe that made him sound like a prick, but it was true. The harder it had been to find Wes, the more he'd wanted him, and that made him an asshole.

When he *had* found him, Wes made it obvious he wasn't interested in a repeat of their night together. It started as a game, hitting on him despite the rejection, just to see Wes fluster. Then Coop dropped the bomb about his dying sister—that Wes had only moved to Blackcreek, Colorado to take care of Chelle and her daughter—and Braden won the 'Asshole of the Year Award' for the way he'd pushed him. Maybe that's what kept him coming around when Wes made it obvious he didn't want him. Braden had two sisters and a brother; it would kill him to lose one of them.

"I know," Cooper said. "But he's Noah's friend, and—"

"Look at you, protecting your boyfriend's friend. If you don't remember, I ended up taking Wes home that night because you went postal thinking he wanted your man."

If he said that to anyone else it probably would have earned him a punch to the jaw, but Cooper knew him. Knew that Braden liked to stir up shit and give people a hard time.

Cooper winked. "It was my plan all along. Was just looking out for ya, man. Helping you get laid, since you obviously can't do it on your own."

"Well played, you bastard." Braden chuckled. When Cooper's boyfriend, Noah, joined them, Braden added, "I'm serious, though, I only want to tell him I'm sorry for his loss, and to be his friend. I'm sure he could use one of those right now."

Noah gave him a small nod before leaning over to kiss the top of Cooper's dark blond hair. "Are you ready to go?" he asked.

"Yeah. Sure."

"Go home and heal your ass up so you can get back to work," Braden teased, making both Cooper and Noah laugh.

"He's milking it. You should see him at home." Noah hooked a finger through Coop's belt loop.

"That's because I'm not stupid. It gets me my way."

Braden had a feeling it didn't take an injury for Noah to do anything for the guy.

"And soon, you'll owe me." Noah's voice went deep, sexy, making Braden see how Cooper, who'd always considered himself straight, had fallen for him.

"See ya later." Noah nodded at him again before leading Cooper away. Braden looked around the small living room to see he was alone. The brown furniture was older but still in good shape. There was a fireplace on the far wall, with a mantel, full of pictures. Braden walked over, his eyes roaming images of Chelle laughing, and Jessie, her little girl, playing. She had a headful of blond curls, much lighter than Wes's dark hair, and his hair was straight.

There were pictures of Wes's other sister, Lydia, who he met for the first time today, with her husband and kids. At the end sat a picture of Wes, leaning against a tree. It was the only image of someone alone.

Braden rubbed a hand across his jaw, studying the picture. Wes's tall, muscular body. The way his head tilted down, showing a jaw that looked like it could cut stone. The jeans hugging his long legs. He really was sexy as hell, and there was no question that he'd been a good fuck, but those things didn't explain why he stood in the man's sister's living room right now.

"Did you need something?" Braden turned at the sound of Wes's lonely voice. "If you haven't noticed, everyone's gone."

Braden smiled at him. "Everyone except me."

He didn't get the return grin he'd hoped for. "Which is my point." Wes crossed his arms.

Damn. This definitely wasn't going to be easy. He figured since they'd gotten along okay while helping Noah when Cooper got hurt, Wes would have gotten over whatever his aversion to Braden was. Obviously not. Braden shrugged. "Thought maybe you'd need some help. Cleaning up or whatever. I'm sure you don't want to deal with that shit right now."

Wes didn't budge. "Lydia and I can take care of it."

"I'm sure she doesn't want to do it, either. It's not a big deal.

I—"

"Why?" Wes interrupted him.

Braden took a few steps toward him. Flirtatious words on the tip of his tongue…*To be alone with you. Because you're sexy as hell.* He fought to find that filter everyone told him he didn't have and answered, "Because my mama raised me to be nice and help people when they need it." Which was true.

Wes's body stiffened so hard, he rivaled marble. "I don't need your pity. If that's—"

"Pity? What are you talking about, man? I can tell you, pity is the last thing I feel when I look at you. If you want, I can prove it to you." As soon as the words left his mouth, he knew he was screwed. Where the fuck had his filter gone?

Braden sighed. "I'm sorry. I didn't come here to hit on you. I just…"

"Uncle Wes! Uncle Wes!" a little girl's voice called, getting closer and closer.

"If you couldn't tell, I'm dealing with shit a whole lot more important than your cock. You can show yourself out." He turned away.

"Wes," Braden called out, but Wes kept going, through the kitchen and toward the back door.

Braden dropped his head back. "Damn it." He'd really fucked that up.

***

Wes paused at the door, closed his eyes, and took a deep breath. The last thing he needed to do today was let something Braden said get under his skin. He got Braden. From the first night they met, he had the guy's number. He'd never had a hard day in his life. Funny, gorgeous, everyone liked him; the kind of man who commanded attention.

He was used to getting what he wanted, and the night they spent together, Wes wanted the same thing Braden did: Sex. Release. And for Wes, a night to forget that Chelle was dying, and that she wanted him to raise Jessie. That once again he was losing someone he loved.

He'd fucked up by leaving before Braden woke up, though. That made him a challenge for Braden, it made him interesting, when Wes didn't want to be interesting to anyone. He had more important things to deal with and didn't have time for playing games.

And he definitely didn't want pity.

"Uncle Wes. Hurry!" Jessie called, her voice all four-year-old happiness. Did she understand the fact that she'd lost her mother forever? She was young, and soon the memories would fade. They always did. She would forget Chelle's smile, her laugh. She wouldn't know what it felt like to have Chelle's unwavering support. She wouldn't have her mom to talk to. She would have... *Wes*.

What had Chelle been thinking by leaving her to him? The single, gay guy who left his job behind to come here, who sucked at opening up to anyone, and had a habit of losing everyone who meant something to him?

Shaking his head, he hoped to leave those thoughts for another time. Wes bound down the stairs for Jessie before the little girl came for him. And she would. She and her mom had had that in common.

Lydia, her husband Stan, and their two sons, Brent and Bruce, sat around the picnic table. Next to it was a swing set so different than the one Wes hung from a tree at home. Chelle had been able to lie on her bed and watch Jessie fly on that homemade swing, though. Now Wes would be watching her on it.

"Push me, Uncle Wes!" Jessie called.

"What? None of you could do it?" Wes winked at his family,

hoping they didn't see his nerves setting him on edge. "Make me come outside when you're all sitting here."

"She wanted you. When Jessie wants something…"

Jessie cut Lydia off with another, "Uncle Wes!"

"I'm coming, I'm coming." Fall leaves crunched under Wes's feet as he walked over to the swing and gave Jessie a push. Lydia had tied Jessie's hair back for her today, but the curls were already springing from the band as she flew through the air. How would he do her hair every day? He didn't even know how.

"Higher! Higher!" she called out.

"I'm trying." Wes hoped his voice sounded lighter than he felt. Behind him, Lydia laughed as Jessie screamed in happiness as he made her fly.

He pushed her for what felt like an hour but was probably closer to fifteen minutes before she finally got tired. When she climbed down, Stan offered to take the kids on a walk, which Wes knew was really an excuse for Lydia to talk to him. They steered clear of the woods behind the house, and walked around to the front. As soon as they disappeared, Lydia asked, "How are you doing?"

He sat across from her, the bench creaking when he did. "I

would guess the same as you. We lost our sister." *Who was more like our mother.*

"You know that's not true, Wes, so don't pretend it is. My heart is broken. I miss her already, but…"

"I'm fine. My loss isn't any bigger than yours."

Her eyes softened, and he knew exactly what they said. That she knew he'd loved Chelle more than anyone in the world. That Chelle was the sister he'd talked to, the first person he'd come out to. He had always assumed he'd have her, and now he didn't.

Lydia's eyes said she worried about him. She worried about Jessie.

"But I don't keep everything locked inside. You've been alone a long time, brother."

He smiled at that.

"She always called you brother. She was so proud to be related to you."

Wes dropped his eyes to the table. He had no idea why, but Chelle had been. She thought the sun rose and set on him, and damned if that hadn't felt good.

After a few minutes of silence, Lydia asked, "Who was the

guy?"

"What guy?" He knew exactly who she meant. Dammit, Braden. He'd caught Lydia's attention.

"You know what guy. He watched you all day."

He had. Wes hadn't wanted to, but he'd watched Braden as well. "And you know who he is. Blackcreek isn't very big, and you've lived here for years."

"Yes, but Braden's only been here less than one."

He raised a brow at her.

"Okay, fine. I know who he is. Why was he watching you? Are you dating him?"

Wes groaned. "Do we really have to do this today?"

Lydia smiled. "He's hot. If I wasn't married, I'd like to date him. Did you see the way his muscles pressed against his shirt? Delicious."

Hearing his sister call a man who Wes spent a night with *delicious*—a man who's muscles he'd bitten his teeth into—was something he could do without ever experiencing again. "I'm not dating him."

"You could, you know." She pushed her hair behind her ear. "I mean, if you're going to be living here, you need to be comfortable. Have a life. You know we support you. Chelle always taught Jessie that love is love."

Wes closed his eyes again, as though that would block out the memories. She'd been just as supportive when he'd come out at sixteen. *It doesn't matter who you love, brother, as long as you love them with your whole damn heart.*

His eyes popped open again. "No offense, but dating is the last thing on my mind right now."

"Don't pretend it's just right now. You haven't dated anyone seriously in years. Don't put it on Chelle's death, or having Jessie."

That was the last thing he wanted to talk about right now. Wes picked at the paint on the table. "I'm not going to do this with you. Braden is…" What was he? He couldn't even say the man was a friend. He'd known him for a couple hours when he went home with him. Then they'd hardly said another word to each other until Cooper got hurt, or rather, Wes had hardly said a word to him. Then it had been all about Cooper and Noah.

But the lack of friendship hadn't stopped Braden from calling him up twice in the past couple weeks. From asking Wes out, and then showing up here today.

"Braden is…?" Lydia asked.

Wes's mind flashed back to the little girl he'd been pushing on the swing. To the niece that he was supposed to raise. To his sister who died, and… "No one. Braden is no one." Those words made him feel like an asshole.

"Fine. I'll drop it. But what about Jessie? She wanted you to have her."

His heart both swelled and broke at those words. "I don't know the first thing about raising a kid, Lydia."

She rolled her eyes. "Who does when they become a parent? It's never what you thought it would be. And you know we'll help you. We're family. We'll do this together." Lydia paused a second before continuing. "You know Jessie can stay with me, but you'll regret it. If you walk away from that little girl, you'll regret it."

"I'm her uncle. I wouldn't be walking away. I'll always be her uncle." Even to his own ears, the excuse sounded weak.

"You know that's not what I mean."

Wes pushed to his feet. "I know. And I'm here, aren't I? You know me better than to think I could ever say no to what Chelle wanted, or to Jessie."

His sister threw herself at him, wrapping her arms around his neck. "We'll figure this out, brother. We'll do it together. It's been too long since you lived close to us. I'm so glad you're here to stay."

And though he loved being around them again, his gut filled with dread. He couldn't let himself screw this up. Couldn't.

Chapter Two

The fire chief eyed Braden from the other side of his desk. He leaned back, trying to decipher what the smirk on his face meant.

"I can't say I'm not disappointed," Bridges raised a brow. "You're a damn good fireman, Roth."

Braden winked at him. "Well, no shit. That's obvious."

The chief laughed. "Which is a little surprising considering that big head you carry on your shoulders. I'm surprised you can hold it up."

Braden stood and held out his hand. "You're a damn good chief, too." He liked working for Bridges. That didn't mean he never wanted to advance, though. Hence the reason Bridges had been looking around a little for him.

Bridges stood, too, and they shook. "Just because this promotion didn't work out doesn't mean the next one won't. I'll let you know if something else comes up."

He nodded. "I know. I'm not in a hurry. Everything's good." They said their goodbyes before Braden walked out. He tossed his bag in the cab of his truck before climbing in and listening to the thing rumble to life. His muscles were dead-tired but his eyes wide awake. He'd always been able to go off not much sleep, probably because he had too much energy for his own good.

Oh, and he hadn't been out in much too long. Cooper used to be his go-to guy when he wanted to go out and find a good time, but now Coop would much rather be home with Noah than anywhere else. Not that Braden could blame him. Well, that was a lie. Braden didn't envy Cooper's situation. He didn't really work that way. He took life as it came to him, too excited about what was to come to want for things he didn't have. But then, sharing a bed with a man like Noah Jameson or Cooper Bradshaw couldn't be a bad thing, either.

I really fucking need to get laid.

Man or woman, he didn't much care about that. Like he'd told Cooper when Cooper first started falling for Noah, the human body was a beautiful thing in all its forms. Braden enjoyed it all.

He glanced at his cell to see it was only 4:30 pm. It wasn't as though he had a whole lot of options to go out this time of day anyway, so he headed to the grocery store to grab a few things.

He made it down two aisles when he noticed a headful of blond, messy curls sticking out from behind a display. Braden felt his lips stretch into a grin as he left his cart next to the meat case and ducked behind the display with her. "Are we hiding?" he asked.

Jessie looked up at him with wide eyes and said, "Uncle Wes is going to put me in karate, that way I can karate-chop strangers if they try to talk to me. I saw you watching Uncle Wes at Mommy's funeral, though. Does that mean you're not a stranger?"

It was Braden's turn for his eyes to go wide. Holy shit. He hadn't even thought about that. "Your uncle is right. You shouldn't talk to strangers." He didn't want her to think he was a stranger. He also didn't want to say he wasn't one, because he sort of was. To her, at least. So what the fuck *did* he say?

Braden settled on, "I wasn't *watching* him." That made it sound like he was panting around the man like a dog or something.

"Yes you were."

"No, I wasn't."

"Yes, you were." Her curls flopped when she nodded. They weren't tied back like they had been when he'd seen her two weeks before.

Jesus, how old was this girl? She argued as well as any woman he'd ever met, and none of his nieces or nephews would notice if a person watched someone or not.

"I was worried about him. That was very nice of me, if I do say so myself." What the hell? How old was *he?* "Are we hiding?" he asked again, trying to change the subject.

"Yep! Uncle Wes doesn't—"

"—Jessie! What are you doing? You can't sneak away from me like that." Wes seemed to pop out of nowhere, grabbing Jessie and pulling her to him. He hugged the little girl tightly.

A heavy weight made Braden's gut sink. Here he'd been trying to play around and hide with her and Wes hadn't known where she was.

"I'm sorry. I was *bored.*" Jessie stepped away.

"It's okay." There was a slight waver to Wes's voice as he tried to smooth her hair down, which just popped back up again.

"Do you got a dog?" Jessie asked Braden, pointing to the dog food in his cart. Wes stood from his kneeling position, unease rolling off him as though he just noticed Braden was standing here.

Braden nodded at him. "I saw her standing here and stopped."

"Thanks…thanks for waiting with her until I found her."

Ummm, or not. He hadn't thought of waiting with her. "No problem." He looked down at Jessie. "I do. He's a chocolate lab, and about as crazy and wild as they come."

"Oooh! I want a puppy. Can we get one, Uncle Wes?" And then to Braden, she asked, "What's his name? Mommy says a name has to mean something."

Wes paled. He briefly closed his eyes and let out a deep breath. Jessie didn't seem to notice, but Braden did. Jessie had said Mommy *says*, not said. His chest ached for the man.

Wes ran a hand through his hair and closed his eyes again, obviously wishing he could disappear.

"His name is Jock." Braden bent down to look Jessie in the eyes, hoping to give Wes a minute.

"What does it mean?"

That he has a fascination with jockstraps… "I'm not creative

19

enough to come up with a name that means something. If I ever get another dog, you can name him. What would you pick?"

She spoke without hesitation. "Uncle Wes."

Above him, he heard Wes chuckle at that. "You can't name a dog after me."

"Why not?" Braden asked at the same time Jessie said, "How come?"

Braden stood. "Personally, I like the name."

Wes crossed his arms. "Nobody asked you."

Jessie pulled on Wes's T-shirt. "That wasn't very nice."

Braden crossed his as well, cocking a brow. He could see the fire in Wes's hazel eyes. He'd seen the same fire the night they'd spent together.

"Yeah, that wasn't very nice." Braden grinned, and Wes's fire blazed even fiercer.

"Mommy says you have to say sorry when you do something that's not very nice." Jessie's big, chestnut eyes looked up at Wes, and Braden knew the man was so incredibly screwed. How would he ever be able to say no to the little girl? And he had to admit, this was a little fun.

What made it better was the small smile threatening to break free across Wes's face. He fought it, that much was obvious, but it wanted to be there. Braden wondered when the last time he smiled was. The night they'd spent together, the only ones he'd shown was when he gave Cooper a hard time about Noah, and he wondered how real those had been.

So this time, he didn't even try and find his filter. Who the hell needed one, anyway? "Apologies go a long way, Uncle Wes. I've been nothing but nice to you." More than once that night, before Wes had bailed on him.

***

Jessie standing next to him was the only thing that kept Wes from strangling Braden. He didn't even care that they were in public. The jail time would be worth wiping that cocky smile from his full lips. Not that his lips were any concern to Wes.

"You're right, Jess. That wasn't very nice of me." His eyes met Braden's, the words much harder to push from his mouth when he did. "I apologize." *I'm going to kill you.*

"I forgot what you said? Why are you sorry?" Braden smirked. Was everything a game to the man?

Wes bit down, trying not to tell Braden what he really felt. The prick. "I apologize for being rude."

Jessie's thin arms wrapped around his waist. "Good job, Uncle Wes."

His heart thudded, suddenly the fake apology becoming worth it. "Thanks, kiddo."

Braden's forehead wrinkled slightly, but then he found his ground. "Yeah, Uncle Wes. Good job. And I forgive you. What are friends for?"

"Stop calling me that. Please." He added the last part so Jessie wouldn't give him hell. She was just as strong and opinionated as her mom had been.

"Oh, can I pick some fruit snacks?" Jessie pointed to the aisle behind them. Wes turned so he could keep an eye on her and nodded. Two seconds later she already ran over, scanning the five million shapes of the same thing.

"You're right." Braden stepped closer to him. Wes stood his ground, not moving backward. That didn't stop Braden from leaning forward, his mouth close to Wes's ear, and whispering, "Considering I've been inside you, that's probably not the best thing to call you."

He tried to pull back, but Wes grabbed his arm and held him there. "I know you're bi, but don't forget who you're talking to. Don't try and flirt with me like you would a woman, because

22

you're not going to get the same response."

With that, Wes walked away. Jessie grabbed her snacks, and when he got to the far end of the aisle, he glanced back. Braden still stood where he'd left him, watching.

Jessie didn't stop talking the whole drive home. When they got to the small, three-bedroom house she'd shared with her mother, they went straight for the kitchen and started cooking tacos, one of the few things he knew how to make. He had a feeling they'd be eating a whole hell of a lot of tacos.

While they cooked, and then through dinner, he searched for the words to talk to Jessie about her mom. Each time he opened his mouth, nothing came out. His chest ached. How was he supposed to do this?

He and Chelle had talked to her before she passed. He and Lydia talked to her after. But she was young. He didn't know if she really got it. Wes wouldn't rely on Lydia every time they needed to have a talk. Jessie was his responsibility, and he damn sure took that seriously.

That didn't make the ache go away, though. Didn't make the words he wished weren't true fall out of his mouth.

"Hey, Jess?"

"Can we watch TV? I wanna watch TV. Will you watch it with me?" she said, her mind always on the go.

"Yeah, yeah, we can watch TV." *Coward.*

They watched a couple episodes of cartoons before he ran a bubble bath for her. One a week, Chelle had said, no more than one bubble bath a week, though he didn't have a clue why. He just knew that her other baths had to be without her favorite part of the whole thing.

He put her in pajamas with feet in them after she finished bathing. She got a package of fruit snacks for her snack, and then Wes said, "It's time for bed, kiddo."

"What 'bout my hair?"

What was wrong with her hair? "Your hair?"

"It's still wet. Mommy says I'm not supposed to go to bed with wet hair when it's getting cold."

"Oh." Wes scratched his forehead. "Okay." He searched the hall bathroom for a blow dryer but couldn't find one. He knew he sure as hell didn't have one in his room, so he checked the hall closet next. It wasn't there, either. Wes looked toward the other end of the house. Toward the closed door he didn't want to go into.

He wanted nothing more than to put her to bed with wet hair, but if Chelle said she couldn't, he wouldn't do that. She'd taken good care of him, and he would do the same thing for her daughter.

"Go in the bathroom and wait for me, okay? I'm going to get the blow dryer."

Jessie skipped to the bathroom, not realizing how close to a heart attack he was. He took a deep breath and just did it. Walked to the other side of the house, opened her door, went straight to the bathroom, ripped the cabinets opened, pulled out the black blow dryer, and then was back out. Had he even taken a breath the whole time he was in there?

There was a distinct scent when someone was dying. He smelled it often at the hospital he used to work at, but had never considered having it in his home. In Chelle's room. It would be gone by now, but he still didn't think he could ever breathe in there again.

It didn't take long to dry her hair. He told her to go to the bathroom again, and waited in her pink bedroom for her to come back. Her hair flew every which way, and he didn't even try to tie it back. He'd almost taken out an eye when he tried this morning.

When Jessie lay under the blankets, Wes sat on the edge of

her bed. "Remember earlier, when we were talking with Braden at the store? You were talking about what your mom said."

Jessie nodded.

His heart felt like someone threw it in a blender and turned it on. "I just wanted to see if you want to talk about her. We always can, you know? That's a good way to remember her." The speed on the blender kicked up. "It's good to talk about her to keep her memory alive. You remember she's not coming back, right?"

He reached out to lay a hand on Jessie's arm, but his fucking hand was shaking. *Hold it together, man. It's your job to hold it together for this little girl.*

Jessie nodded. No words, just a nod.

"It's okay to miss her."

"Do you miss her?" Jessie asked.

He closed his eyes and focused on trying to slow his heartbeat. "I do."

"Me, too." She turned on her side, and this time he kept his hand steady as he pushed her hair away from her face.

"She loved you more than anything, kiddo."

"You, too. Mommy said family is the most 'portant thing in the world."

He smiled at how she said 'important.' "It is. You okay?"

Jessie nodded. Wes leaned forward and pressed a kiss to her forehead. "Good night, Jess."

He got all the way to the door before her voice stopped him. "Is Braden a stranger?"

Wes squeezed the doorknob. "No…not really."

"He's your friend, though. He was at Aunt Lydia's for Mommy's funeral."

He let the question roll around in his head. She had enough going on in her life; he didn't want her to be confused about Braden, too. "Yeah, yeah, he's a friend. We have lots of friends, though. The people in your preschool class, and Noah and Cooper. You remember them?"

Jessie nodded. "I'm glad he's our friend. I like him. I didn't want to have to karate-chop him."

Wes laughed, some of the tension in his chest dropping off with it. But then he thought of Braden's last words to him. Jessie didn't have to worry about karate-chopping him, because Wes would probably kill the man first.

Maybe that would take his kissable lips, and his rough, skilled hands out of Wes's mind. Because as much as he didn't want to admit it, they'd been there since the night he'd walked out on Braden.

Chapter Three

The next morning Braden kicked back in his recliner and dialed his phone. There was a second where he wondered if maybe he shouldn't do it, but hesitation wasn't really how he worked. What did you ever gain by holding back? He had something to say, and he damn sure planned to say it.

Wes, on the other hand, probably wouldn't agree with him.

Braden grinned when Wes answered on the third ring. "What do you want?"

"You answered."

"Isn't that what I'm supposed to do when someone calls?"

Huh. That reply hadn't been one he expected. "You've

ignored my calls before."

"Would you rather I hang up? I can do that. It's not like I don't have other things to do." The tone of Wes's voice had that edge of sexy seriousness it always did. It drove Braden wild, which he didn't get at all. He usually didn't go for serious.

"No, don't hang up. You're not going to want to miss this." Braden flipped the button closing his recliner before heading to the kitchen. "I'm calling to apologize. I hope you realize how rare an occasion this is. In fact, I can hold on if you want to record it or dictate the conversation or something."

Silence greeted him.

"Ah fuck. I didn't make you pass out, did I?"

A husky chuckle came through the phone, making Braden smile. That might be the first time he'd heard Wes laugh.

"You're crazy."

Braden leaned against his kitchen counter and crossed his arms. "Does that mean I'm forgiven?" When Wes didn't reply right away, he added, "I'm only apologizing for what I said at the end of the service. It's true, but my timing was wrong. And also for the grocery store yesterday. My doctor is still trying to come up with a cure for my 'open mouth, insert foot' disorder."

He listened for a minute to the sound of Wes breathing through the phone before the man finally answered. "If we're being honest, let's admit that you have no real reason to apologize. I do, though. Things have just been…"

Braden waited for him to continue but he didn't. And it didn't surprise Braden, either. He didn't know much about Wes, but it was obvious he kept most things to himself. That had never bothered Braden about anyone before, yet even though he understood it, it still felt like that annoying itch he couldn't scratch. What did Wes have against talking to him? "It's cool, man. You're going through a lot. I get it. We can be friends. I know how to only be friends, ya know."

Wes gave another of his signature pauses. While he waited, Braden thought about telling Wes he liked the new facial hair he had at the store yesterday. Not a full goatee, but dark hair on his chin that added to his sexiness. Luckily, he found it in himself to keep quiet.

"Listen, I better go. I need to pick Jessie up from preschool in a little while, and I have some things to take care of first," Wes finally said.

A deep breath pushed from Braden's lungs. There was his answer, he guessed. "Alright. Have a good one."

He pulled the phone from his ear, about to hit end, when Wes's voice stopped him. "Thanks…thanks for calling."

Before Braden could reply, the man hung up. Damned if Braden wasn't smiling again. He wasn't sure why Wes's words made him feel so good.

A couple days later, Braden jumped into his truck and headed over to Cooper's house. Braden had the day off and he was bored as hell. Since Noah worked today, and Coop wasn't back to the firehouse yet, they'd decided to hang out.

His buddy answered the door quickly. "Where's the sling?" Braden asked.

"Fuck off," was Coop's reply, and Braden couldn't help but laugh.

"Bet you wear it when Noah's around." Noah was a good guy, and obviously crazy in love with Cooper. Braden didn't know him too well, but he did know that if the doc still wanted Coop in that sling, Noah would make damn sure he had it on while around.

"Again, fuck off. It's driving me batty. I'm starting rehab on my arm this week. If I can handle that, I can handle not wearing the thing for a few hours."

Braden laughed at Coop's surly voice as he followed him into the living room. Cooper sat in the chair and Braden the couch. "It's driving you bat-shit crazy not being at work, isn't it?" he asked.

"Yeah, I miss it. I need to get my ass back out there. I'm driving Noah crazy, too."

Braden nodded, because he got it. He always needed to keep busy. If he wasn't working, he needed to be doing something. He played on a local soccer team, worked out a lot, and *went* out a lot, too.

As a kid his mom always used to say he spent all his time looking for the next best thing. That wasn't really what it boiled down to, though. He just hadn't found anything that held his attention for long. Wasn't his fault. "I'm sure you're not driving Noah crazy."

Cooper cocked a brow at him. "What about you? Are you driving Wes crazy?"

"Not even close to the same thing, man." Braden still couldn't pinpoint exactly what the fascination with Wes really was. There was something about him that made Braden curious, though— made him wonder about the distance Wes had in his eyes, despite the big heart he obviously had. Braden saw it when he looked at Jessie, saw it when he helped Noah and Cooper out, yet when it came to himself, he always pulled back.

There was that part of him that just wanted to push the more Wes tried to pull, though. His mom would give him hell for that. His parents were still happily married after almost forty years. His siblings were all happily hitched, but again, he'd never met someone who held his interest, despite how much his mom wanted him to.

He'd never had a relationship that lasted longer than a couple months, and even then he'd only had two. The longest lasting had been Gavin. They dated when he was eighteen, but were much better as friends.

He was twenty-nine years old, and since he moved from home at eighteen, he'd lived in four different states. He just hadn't found anything that made him want to stick.

Cooper grinned. "That doesn't mean you're not driving him crazy."

Shaking his head, Braden replied, "Fuck off. What's the point if it's not the kind of crazy that leaves us both sweaty in bed together?"

"So move on."

Move on? What the hell did he mean by that? "It's not like I'm stuck on him. I'm not waiting around for him, either. Just because you went and fell in love, don't start looking for it everywhere else."

Cooper laughed. "I'm giving you shit. But you have to admit you haven't been going out as much."

Picking up a magazine from the table beside him, Braden threw it at Cooper. "That's because my dumbass friend nearly got himself killed, and then I was trying to be a friend to Wes. He lost his sister and gained a kid. Gotta be tough." He'd talked to Wes one other time since he apologized, having called him up to check in. He wasn't kidding when he said that's how his mama raised him. You were there for your friends; at least, Braden was.

"Now can we shut the hell up and turn some sports on or something? You need to get your ass back to work to keep yourself busy. You're turning into a damn gossip."

Coop laughed and hit the power button on the remote.

"And just so you know, I'm going out tonight." Cooper was right. He hadn't been out in too long. It was time to change that.

***

"What am I supposed to do, Lydia? I have an interview in an hour. I need to get a job. We have bills to pay." Wes paced the living room, his heart dangerously close to breaking through his rib cage.

"Don't get an attitude with me. I didn't know you had an interview today, and it's no one's fault she's sick. I can talk to my boss and see if I can get off. We're shorthanded today, though. You might have to reschedule."

Because rescheduling a job interview was a great idea. It wasn't as though Blackcreek and the surrounding areas had a plethora of hospitals for him to choose from. "Dammit. Why did she have to get sick today? I did everything right. I scheduled the appointment when she'd be in preschool!" He'd wanted to do this without help. He could have tried for the afternoon when Lydia would be off work and could watch Jessie, but Chelle had left Jessie to him, not Lydia. He wanted to do right by her, and the first time he tried, things got fucked up.

Wes fell into the chair, elbows on his knees, leaning his head into his hands.

"These things happen. I know it's tough, but it's part of being a parent. Let me talk to my boss. I'll see if I can leave early. You're doing a good job, Wes."

Yeah, he wasn't so sure of that. "No. It's not fair for you to have to figure this out. I'll...I'll take care of it."

Wes ended the call, rolling his cell around in his hand. A low cough came from the bedroom and he jogged over, peeking in to see Jessie still sleeping. Maybe he should cancel the interview. What if she needed to go to the doctor? What if she was *really* sick?

He shook those thoughts from his head. Her fever was only one hundred point four when he'd given her medicine. Lydia would have told him if he needed to take her in.

That didn't help him with the interview, though.

Wes went back down the hall. Fuck the job. Jessie was more important. If they didn't understand, then he probably wouldn't do well working for them anyway.

Though he guessed he could ask Noah. He trusted him with Jessie. Jess did well with just about anyone. Noah was really the only person he knew well enough to want to leave Jessie with. They didn't come more responsible than him.

He tried Noah's cell first but he didn't answer. Their home phone rang for times before, "Cooper and Noah's love shack."

"You dumbass!" Cooper yelled as Wes said, "Braden?"

"Aw, miss me did, ya? Calling all around town looking for me?" Braden asked, his voice a mixture of sex and humor.

"I don't have time to play games. Is Noah around?"

"He's at work. What's wrong?" Braden spoke much more seriously that time.

"I have a job interview in forty-five minutes. It's a thirty-minute drive. Jessie's sick, Lydia's working, and now Noah is, too. Fuck!" He'd only been at this a few weeks and he already didn't know what to do. Wes leaned against the wall, dropping his head back to rest on it.

"Gimme ten and I'll be there."

At Braden's words, he jerked his eyes open. "You just answered the phone 'Noah and Cooper's love shack' and now you want to babysit my sick niece?"

"Actually, I said Cooper and Noah, but yeah. And too bad for you, you don't have time to argue." The line went dead.

Wes squeezed the cell in his palm, almost throwing it across the room. Couldn't one fucking thing go right?

He shoved his feet into his shoes and went to the bathroom to fix his tie, hoping the distraction would help him forget that he had no choice but to leave Jessie with Braden Roth.

A few minutes later there was a knock at the door. It wasn't until he opened it that he realized he'd never told Braden where he lived. "How'd you know where our house was?"

Braden slipped inside, brushing against Wes as he did. He wore a long-sleeved shirt, camo, with a leather necklace around his neck. For some reason, Wes wondered if he wore the black leather bracelets that he usually had on his wrists. He couldn't see because of his shirt. But he did notice the scent of soap drifting around Wes when Braden passed.

"I asked Coop, who had to call Noah at the shop. I drove, he called me with the address as I did, and abracadabra, I'm here. Where's the Squirt?" He crossed his arms, looking completely comfortable leaning against Wes's deep green couch.

How in the hell did they get here? He'd fucked this man after knowing him for an hour, and now he would babysit Jess? *He's Cooper's friend. He works for the fire department.* He could trust him.

"She's in the second room down the hall. She's sleeping right now. Maybe go check on her like every ten minutes or so. I gave her medicine two hours ago. She gets a teaspoon every four hours, but only if she's not feeling well or has a fever. It's on the bathroom counter. I'll keep my phone on vibrate. Text me every little while to let me know how she's doing. If you need me, call. I don't give a shit if she just has a runny nose and wants to talk to me. Call."

It wasn't till he finished talking that he realized the right side of Braden's mouth kicked up in a partial smile. Dark stubble, matching his chocolate brown hair, teased his jawline. Fucker. Why did he have to be so sexy? "What?"

"I have six nieces and nephews. I can handle it. You better go before you're late." Braden crossed his arms, his deltoids flexing when he did. Wes loved those damn muscles. They'd always been his favorite.

Braden's smile grew. "Aren't you running short on time?"

Wes shook his head, adjusted his tie again. Yeah, he needed to go. Go to his interview so he had money to take care of his niece, who slept in the next room. These were the things he needed to focus on. "I'll be back as soon as I can."

He turned toward the door when Braden's voice stopped him. "Wes."

He looked back. "What?"

"The suit? Holy shit, what I can imagine doing to you in that thing. You look good."

Wes closed his eyes. He couldn't do this right now. Really couldn't. Maybe not ever. He wasn't good at this kind of thing. Didn't really know how to open his mouth and accept the compliment. And at this time in his life, dealing with a man wasn't something he needed to worry about. Not that he even knew what he'd say regardless.

Wes opened his eyes and turned for the door again. This time he got as far as opening it before Braden called his name again.

"What?" Wes groaned out, this time without turning around.

"You're doing real good with her. Just thought you should know."

His fist tightened on the doorknob. He wanted nothing more than to do right by that little girl. The words *thank you* lodged in his throat; not because he had a problem thanking someone, but because Braden's words meant something to him. They made his chest fill and blood rush through him.

Everyone who knew him understood how hard it was for him to talk about things that really mattered. If he didn't say them, he could pretend they weren't true. Not feeling made it a whole lot easier when he lost them, and Wes always lost the people who mattered to him.

"Tick tock, man. You're going to be late." Braden saved him. Wes took the life raft he tossed and walked out without another word.

Chapter Four

Quietly, Braden slipped down the hallway for his fourth fifteen-minute check of Jessie. Fifteen minutes he could do. Wes's suggestion of every ten was just crazy.

He pushed the door open to see her lying on her side with her eyes open. "Hey Squirt. You remember me, right?"

She nodded. "You're Braden, and you're not a stranger. I asked Uncle Wes."

That made him smile. He wasn't a stranger, huh? He had a feeling even something as small as telling Jessie that had been tough for Wes. "Your uncle had to go somewhere very important. He'll be back in about an hour, though. How ya feeling?" Braden stepped into the room.

"Okay."

He stopped next to her bed and saw a thermometer there. "Do you think we should take your temperature real quick?"

She nodded, looking much more puny than she had at the grocery store the other day. He told her to lift her tongue and he put the thermometer into her mouth. When it beeped, he saw her temperature was ninety-nine point nine. Not bad at all.

"Can I watch TV?" Jessie asked him.

"Sure." TV sounded like a better idea than thinking about Wes, which is what he'd been doing before she woke up. Wes's rambling step-by-step instructions on taking care of Jessie had been cute. Wes was already a good father to her, yet he didn't see it. Braden couldn't understand how he couldn't. Those little things intrigued him, made him want to know what made Wes tick and why.

Braden helped her up, grabbing her blanket and pillow. He made her a bed on the couch and turned on the TV. She snuggled under her princess blanket as he flipped through the channels.

"Nice. Tom and Jerry is on," he said, and she wrinkled her nose at him. "Is that a 'I don't like Tom and Jerry' frown, or an 'I've never seen Tom and Jerry' frown?"

"I only watch princesses or Disney."

Oops. Tom and Jerry wasn't bad, was it? "Because you aren't supposed to watch other things, or because you only like those things?"

"Princesses are pretty."

That was a good enough answer to him. "How about we watch one episode, and if you don't laugh like crazy, I'll turn it. Deal?" He held out his hand to her but Jessie just smiled in response.

"Mommy paints my nails when I'm sick. Can you paint my nails?"

Umm, did he have to? "Are you bribing me into painting your nails so I can watch Tom and Jerry?" Braden tried not to laugh but couldn't help himself. She was good.

His laughter died when she asked, "What's that?"

Nice. Wes left him with her for two hours and he almost taught her how to start bribing people to get her way. "Nothing. Where's the nail polish?"

He looked in the bathroom cabinet like she said and found about eleven thousand shades of pink. He grabbed two of them and took them out so Jessie could pick. As it turned out, she wanted both. He set them on the coffee table and sat down on the floor in front of her. Jessie stretched her arm out toward him, all messy curls and red cheeks.

"You're enjoying this too much," he teased as he opened the bottles. As he did, Jerry snagged Tom in one of Tom's own traps and they both started laughing. "You haven't seen the best of it yet. Keep watching."

Jessie giggled, her eyes on the TV.

Braden wasn't going to pretend he knew the first thing about painting nails. What he did learn was wiping the brush was a must, because her first nail had polish halfway down her finger.

She didn't seem to mind, though, just lay there watching Tom and Jerry. Every so often he'd forget what he was doing and get lost in cat and mouse antics, but then Jessie would wiggle her fingers again and he would start painting.

The door opened while he painted her last nail. *Fuck.* He'd hoped to finish before Wes got back. The man stood in the doorway, looking down at Braden on the floor with two colors of bright-pink nail polish open next to him.

"Tom and Jerry's on." Braden winked at Wes, which seemed to wake him up.

"I see that. And you're painting nails."

"I have two sisters."

"I had two sisters as well, and I've never painted a nail in my life."

Braden shook his head while Wes smiled. He closed the door and walked over, laying a hand on Jessie's forehead. "How ya doing, kiddo?"

"Good."

Braden closed the bottles and stood. "I didn't give her anything. Her fever's only ninety-nine point nine. I haven't checked in a bit, though. You might want to."

He noticed Wes had loosened his tie, leaving it draped around his neck. The urge to grab it and pull him closer made Braden's palms tingle but he held back.

"You get the job?" he asked.

Wes's eyebrows rose playfully, something Braden had never seen from the man. "Nailed it."

Oh, the things he could say to that comment. Wes seemed to realize it, because he added, "You say it and I'm kicking your ass."

"That's not nice, Uncle Wes!" Jessie called from the couch.

Wes's jaw tightened.

"Smart kid." Braden chuckled.

"You're always taking his side." He ruffled Jessie's hair. Braden watched his eyes when he looked at her, saw how much he loved her, but the fear there, too. Damn, he respected the man. He wanted him again, too, but now probably wasn't the best time to be thinking about that.

"Well, I guess I'll let you guys get back to your day. You get better Squirt, okay?" Braden waved at her and took a step back. When he did, Jessie sat up.

"Don't go. Can't you stay? I bet Uncle Wes hasn't seen Tom and Jerry, either. We can all watch. And I'm hungry. Do we have anything to eat? Popsicles, too. Mommy says the only time you can eat as many popsicles as you want is when you're sick."

Wow. That was a mouthful. Braden looked at Wes. "How do you keep up with her?"

Wes had his eyes firmly on Jessie. "I'm sure Braden has things to do."

"Please, Uncle Wes. Please, Braden!" Jessie asked before she started coughing again.

Wes knelt beside her, stroking her hair. "Please Uncle Wes?" she asked again.

Braden heard Wes exhale, but then he looked up at Braden, question in his eyes. "Sure, Squirt. I can stay. Only if you have popsicles, though." Hanging out with them sounded more fun than anything else he could think of anyway.

***

Wes set the bags of groceries on the counter as Braden slipped into the kitchen behind him. "She fell asleep again. I left her on the couch. I didn't know if I should carry her to her room or if leaving her there would be okay."

"She's good where she is." He kept his voice low as not to wake her. "Since she's sleeping, you can head out if you want. I don't want to keep you." Being Friday, Braden probably had plans tonight.

"Nah. I promised the kid I'd make her chicken soup, so I will. It was my mom's staple when we were sick. Unless you want me to go?" Braden cocked a brow at him. He always did that. It shouldn't be so sexy, but it was.

He also should tell Braden to leave. The man had no business being tied into their lives. He didn't want Jessie to get close to someone who had no reason to stick around. "Listen," Wes peeked into the living room to see she still slept. "This is probably going to make me sound like an ass, which I'm sure wouldn't be a surprise to you considering I have a habit of it, but we have a lot of shit going on right now. She lost her mom. I don't know the first thing about raising a kid. I don't have time in my life for anything else." All the truth, but what Braden didn't know was that he never had time for anything else. Lydia had been right about that.

It took a minute for Braden to reply. He stepped close to Wes and fingered his tie. Heat scorched through him that easily. Damn the man and the physical response he had over Wes.

"I know I gave you hell before, but I get it. It's never really happened to me before, but you apparently have more important things in your life than fucking me."

Wes laughed. "Always joking around."

"Not when it's important. I know the difference. Just friends." He held up two fingers. "Scouts honor."

"Don't they hold up three fingers?"

"Don't know. Never was a scout." He grabbed Wes's tie again and yanked. Wes went easily, cursing himself the whole time. His body lined up flush against Braden's. He smelled the man's soap again and felt Braden's body heat seeping into him.

He lowered his lips so they were close to Wes's ear, and damned if his cock didn't start to stir.

"Sorry. That fucking tie was killing me. Just wanted to do that once. *Now* just friends. Scouts honor." He let go and stepped back.

A small tingle of anger formed in Wes's gut, but it wasn't stronger than his amusement. "You would have made a shitty boy scout."

Braden winked. "For more than one reason."

Wes had no doubt about that.

Jessie slept on and off all afternoon. Braden made chicken soup, something Wes never would have expected, before getting sent back to the store for popsicles.

Jess drank a little of the broth but that was all. Mostly she and Braden ate popsicles all day and watched cartoons. Hours passed, and Wes expected Braden to leave at any time but he didn't.

The afternoon flew by faster than he expected. By seven that evening, Jessie was ready for bed.

It didn't take Wes long to get her ready. He slipped her bedroom door closed and went into the living room to hear the water running. "Hey. You don't need to do the dishes. You cooked."

Braden shrugged. "I get antsy if I'm sitting around too much. It's no problem."

"That go for your personal life, too?" he asked, not sure why he did. To distract himself, he went over and started filling the dishwasher as Braden rinsed.

"I guess. I get bored easily. Always have. There's a big world out there, and I don't want to miss anything, ya know?"

No, he really didn't. He'd never had his head in the clouds, never really wanted a whole lot. They hadn't had much growing up. As long as he had his family, he'd been okay. His dad had been like that, though, which was why he left and never came back.

"So that's why you swing both ways. Just one bores you?" Wes turned off the water and leaned against the counter. It was another question he shouldn't be curious about.

"No, not really. I mean, in one way, you could look at it like that. If something feels good, I do it. Why not? But then, it's not like I get bored of a woman so I go in search of a man, or the other way around. I'm attracted to people because of how they make me feel. I'm attracted to who they are—the person, and not their gender."

Wes nodded, though he didn't really get it. It wasn't as if they should be talking sex anyway, so he said, "Thanks for cooking. I'm shit in the kitchen."

Braden winked. "I'm a man of many talents."

Yeah, he remembered.

"What do you do?" Braden asked, leaning back on the counter as well.

"What?"

"For a job. I don't even know what you do."

Damn, this whole thing was ass backward. They'd fucked, and now Braden spent the day cooking and helping him take care of his niece, yet he didn't even know what Wes did for a living?

"I'm a respiratory therapist."

"You like it?"

"Yeah, I guess. Wanted to be a doctor, but this is okay." Most people would probably give Braden more there. Say why he hadn't tried to do what he wanted, but he'd never really worked that way. It used to drive his ex, Alexander, crazy. He'd told him so when he left Wes.

Braden sighed, and Wes wondered if he saw that already. Saw that Wes really was shit to have for a friend and definitely not good at anything more than that. That made sense, anyway. He might as well see how Wes was up front.

"I'm going to head out." Braden stepped away from the sink but then stopped. "She's a cool kid. I work three twelves, so I'm around four days a week. If you ever need help with her again, I'm around."

"I'll be working three twelves, too. I don't know my days yet, but Lydia can usually pick her up from preschool. We only had a problem today because of being sick."

Braden nodded and started for the door. Wes went behind him, telling himself it was just because he needed to lock up. Like Wes had earlier, Braden got as far as putting a hand on the doorknob before Wes's voice stopped him. "Thanks. For helping out today. For rushing over here and…hell, for helping me at all. I know I've been a prick."

Braden turned toward him. He had fire in his eyes. His square jaw sexy as hell, with that fucking hair Wes loved. He didn't know which of them moved first—maybe both of them—but suddenly Braden's mouth was on his and Wes pushed his tongue in, wanting nothing more than to taste him.

Hands were everywhere, Braden's up the back of Wes's shirt, hot callused hands against his flesh. Wes wrapped his arms around Braden, digging into Braden's shoulder muscles that he'd been admiring earlier.

Braden's mouth ripped from his, sliding down before his teeth bit into Wes's neck. "Fuck, I've wanted to do this again since the last time."

As much as he hated it, he had, too. *This* he could give—sex, release. But this time, this time he wanted Braden. He wanted to be the one doing the fucking.

Wes pushed him backward. Braden laughed as he hit the door, grabbing Wes and pulling Wes with him.

Their mouths fused together again when Jessie's shaky voice broke through the haze. "Uncle Wes! I threw up!"

Wes jerked back. Fuck. *Fuck!* What had he been thinking?

"Shit. I wasn't thinking. I'm sorry," Braden said. "Want me to help with her?"

Wes didn't realize he was already walking away until he stopped to reply to Braden. "I got it. You can go." He almost went for Jessie again but added, "I appreciate it, though." Because he did. When he met the man, he'd assumed Braden was a flake. He seemed to coast through life just having fun, but the fact that he was here said a lot. The fact that he offered to help when Wes's niece vomited said a lot. Damn it all to hell, because there was more to Braden then he'd realized. This would be a whole lot easier if there wasn't.

Chapter Five

Braden ripped off his helmet and fell into place on the fire truck. His gloves came next before he dropped his head back against the side of the truck.

That had been a close one, a really fucking close one to get those people out before the building collapsed around them. He still felt the lingering effects of the heat. Adrenaline still pumped through his body, making his leg bounce up and down.

They'd done it. That was all that mattered to him. But like it always did after a fire, his body felt amped up even more than usual. Like he couldn't catch up with himself. He still felt the woman's body in his arms, high on the fact that he'd gotten her out because nothing else had been an option.

"Good job in there today, Roth," Charlie, one of the men in his crew, said.

"Just doing my job." He leaned a little as the truck took a corner.

It didn't take them long to get back to the station. They took care of business, and a few hours later, he climbed into his truck after work. He should be dead on his feet. In a way he was, but that's not really how Braden worked. There was no way he could rest and recoup tonight. His body still hadn't shut down from the day.

When Charlie came out after him, Braden rolled down the window and called out, "Want to go grab a drink or something?"

Charlie shook his head. "Nah. Sarah would kick my ass."

Braden chuckled. "You guys are back on this week, then?" They were always breaking up and getting back together. He couldn't keep up with their relationship, not that he tried to.

"For good this time. We're getting married."

"No shit?"

Charlie nodded. "She always spoils my ass when there's a big fire. Not missing out on it to have drinks with you."

Braden couldn't blame him. Instead of saying goodbye, he grinned, shook his head, and rolled the window up again, missing the cool air when he did. He loved fall in Colorado. Loved the slight crispness in the air. Not that you could always count on the weather there, but when it was like now, he thrived. Cool, sunny days and cold nights.

Braden picked up his phone and thought about calling to check on Jessie. He hadn't spoken to Wes since he left his house a few nights ago. Hopefully the little girl felt better. She was a cool kid. He'd had a good time with her, and he definitely had a good time with Wes, even if he did make Braden swear to be a boy scout and then kissed the hell out of him afterward.

He really, really wanted to fuck the man again—or let Wes fuck him. He didn't much care which way they went, but then he thought about that little girl again and everything Wes was dealing with and that made him feel like an asshole. He couldn't imagine that kind of responsibility. Jock was enough for him. His dog, or when he stayed with one of his siblings to watch his nieces or nephews for a night.

Friends or not, their attraction for each other would make things difficult, and as much as he wanted Wes, he didn't want to make things harder on him.

So instead of calling Wes, he dialed Coop to see if maybe he and Noah wanted to go have a few beers with him tonight.

"Cooper and Noah's love shack," Coop teased when he answered the phone.

"It doesn't sound nearly as good when you're saying it instead of me."

"How'd babysitting duty go the other night?" Cooper asked.

"I painted nails."

"Whoa. TMI. Wes is a kinky bastard, huh?"

Braden laughed. "Jessie's nails, smart guy."

"Oh, yeah. Okay." Cooper pretended he didn't know what Braden meant.

"I should have called your boyfriend instead of you. He's the more levelheaded one. Ask Noah if he wants to go shoot some pool with me tonight."

"Funny. Didn't get enough the other night?"

"Nah, I didn't end up going. I hung out with Jessie and Wes for a while, and then I was tired so I just went home."

Coop paused for a minute before replying. "Sounds like things are better with you guys. We're going to Wes's for that party he's having to celebrate his new job. Why aren't you?"

Braden felt a little sting in his chest. Wes planned a party for tonight? That didn't sound like something he would do at all. And he obviously hadn't wanted Braden there, since this was the first he heard about it. "Wasn't invited." It shouldn't matter, it really shouldn't, and in a lot of ways, it didn't. In all honesty, though, he called them friends. Were they really? He didn't even know Wes. They'd fucked once, and now they could put it behind them. And in reality, neither of them owed the other anything; especially something like inviting the other to a party. But he'd also thought that after the other day, things would change. Maybe they *would* be friends.

"Shit. I figured since you guys hung out the other day, you came to some kind of understanding."

Yeah. Cooper and him both. "It doesn't matter. I'll just go out tonight like I planned. I'm a big boy. I'm not going to get my heart broken because some guy I had sex with didn't invite me to a party." And he wouldn't, but damned if that little sting in his chest still wasn't there.

***

"I really don't get why we needed to do this, Lyd." Wes

crossed his arms and leaned against the back of the couch.

Lydia swatted at his hands. "You always stand like that, like you're mad at the world or something. Was your life really that hard?" She held no anger in her voice…just curiosity blended with sadness.

And in reality, he agreed with what she said. No, his life hadn't been too hard. His dad had bailed, but how many people dealt with that? His mom would have done anything for them, even go as far as working two jobs to take care of them. And it was that love that had killed her. Her tired eyes that just wanted a few seconds reprieve, and it had been enough to veer into another lane and get hit head on.

It had broken all three of them to lose her…but then he'd always had Chelle. Until they lost her, too. Just like he'd lost the only man he'd ever loved. The difference there being that Alexander had chosen to walk away. *Can I blame him?*

"You know it wasn't that hard. Regardless, that has nothing to do with my not wanting to have a party." Hosting people at his home was just not the kind of man he'd ever been.

Lydia sighed. "We haven't had a lot to celebrate. Why not grab on to whatever we can?"

He closed his eyes, knowing she was right but not able to find the words to tell her.

"We need to try and get back to life as normal for Jessie. She's a people person just like her mama, and you know Chelle loved hosting parties. It's something fun for her, to make her feel some normalcy."

Wes frowned. "Way to make me feel like an ass, Lyd."

She grinned, and he pulled her to him and gave her a hug.

"You've always been so serious, Wes. You're responsible, and you always do the right thing. Have some fun. Loosen up. You deserve to be happy. Do you even still paint anymore?"

He hadn't painted for a long time. He wasn't even sure why. He ignored that question and said, "I'm happy." And he was, in most ways. He had a career he loved. Maybe not his dream job, but he enjoyed what he did, enjoyed helping people. He had Jessie, and he loved the little girl more than anything. Just because that was enough for him—those certainties didn't mean he wasn't happy.

"You should share it a little more, then. Some of us would like to see it from you." She nudged him. "Is the hottie coming?"

"Ah, hell. Not this again. What is it with women trying to be matchmakers for gay men? I don't have a problem getting men when I want them. And that's the end of this conversation." Wes took a step away but Lydia grabbed his arm.

"I'm not trying to play matchmaker for a gay man, I'm just trying to keep my brother from doing his damndest to make sure he's always alone. The risk of losing people is sometimes worth it."

Not to him. "How did we get from a party to relationships?" Before she could answer him, the doorbell rang and Wes pulled away to answer it.

A couple hours later about twenty people filled his living room. They were all people Lydia knew. He got it. She wanted him to meet people, to make himself at home more in Blackcreek. He needed to do it, for Jessie, at least. That didn't mean he thought this was fun, though.

"You like corners." Noah stepped up beside him. "Sometimes I find it funny that you're the one who approached me that night."

Wes shrugged. "You know what they say, the dick is mightier than…hell, just about anything else."

Noah laughed. "That it is, man. How you doing?"

"About as good as can be expected. I'm ready to get to work. I think it will help. It's something that's normal for Jess, ya know? Trying to show her that life keeps moving."

Nodding, Noah said, "Speaking of Jessie, I heard Braden babysat. The house is still standing, I see. And he even missed a night of going out."

Wes's head whipped in Noah's direction at that. He'd had plans? But that didn't make sense. Braden babysat during the day and left around seven. "What makes you say that?"

"He asked Coop to go out, but then went to watch Jessie when you called. Sorry I wasn't around, by the way. I know he didn't end up going after he left. It's strange," he laughed. "They're like a couple of gossiping women, sometimes."

Wes almost mentioned that they were practically doing the same thing, but instead he let himself think about the fact that, going out or not, Braden had dropped everything to help Wes out. And he's stayed long after he had to. "Can you excuse me for a second?" Wes already began walking away before Noah could reply. He made it all the way to his room and closed the door before he started dialing.

"I'm looking to buy some Boy Scout cookies. You're the only one I know who can get them…Can you come over?"

Braden laughed. "Boy scouts don't sell cookies, asshole."

"They don't?"

"No."

"I guess I'm not the only one who would make a bad scout, not that they'd let me in, or as though I'd want to be there anyway." He paused, knowing he should give a real reason for asking him over, for keeping the party from him in the first place. That he should make sure Braden knew he appreciated his help with Jessie the other day. But that damned block he had inside him kept the words at bay. "I know Jessie would really like to meet Jock."

Braden sighed, making Wes think he might say no, making him realize he wanted Braden to say yes.

"I wouldn't want to disappoint the Squirt. We'll be there soon."

Chapter Six

Jock danced around in the seat next to him, stoked to be going somewhere. He pressed his nose against the window, obviously wanting to stick his head out.

"It's cold, buddy." Braden petted his brown head as he drove toward Wes's house. Not that Jock cared about the chill. He just loved being outside, loved playing.

And here Braden was analyzing the behavior of his dog so he didn't think about the fact that it made him happy that Wes called. The man just had something about him that intrigued Braden. Even from the first night they'd met, he'd been drunk and had obviously enjoyed getting under Cooper's skin. He'd purposely needled Coop where Noah was concerned, and Braden would be lying if he didn't admit that it had been a little funny.

In bed, he'd been just what Braden enjoyed—rough, and passionate. Verbal about what he wanted, and what he wanted done to him. A man who wanted to be fucked and wasn't afraid to ask for it, but also who made that slow-burn curl at the base of Braden's spine, making him wonder what it would be like to be taken by him, too.

They'd been at a bar with Noah and Cooper that night, and despite Wes's prickly behavior with Coop, more lingered right below the surface—pain, anger and loneliness. He'd sensed it then, and he definitely saw it now. He hid it well, but for those who took the time to look, you saw it.

The only time it disappeared is when they were in bed together. It felt like the only time Wes took something just for himself. For someone like Braden, that interested him. He didn't quite understand it, and wasn't sure why he wanted to. It was more than just being a challenge, though; Wes just plain caught his attention.

After pulling into Wes's driveway, he killed the engine, grabbed Jock's ball and stepped out of the truck. He snapped his fingers. "Stay with me, boy," he said to Jock, who trotted next to him, practically bursting from the seams to run.

It took a few minutes for the door to open after he knocked. Wes's sister, Lydia, stood on the other side. The woman flashed him a million-watt smile. She definitely wasn't happy to see him for the same reason most women were.

"Braden, hi. I didn't know you were coming. Not that I didn't want you to. I do, we do. I just didn't know."

He grinned and her cheeks flushed.

"I'm rambling. Sorry. Please come in."

Jock didn't leave his side as he stepped in the door. People stood in different groups around the room. Chips, dip and other food sat on the kitchen table.

"The best way to find Wes is to search the corners." She laughed, but it sounded forced.

"I'll drag him out. Even if it's just because I'm driving him crazy." Braden winked at her, excitement skittering through him. He liked getting under Wes's skin. Liked being the one to fluster him both sexually and by plain frustrating him.

"You seem to know my brother," Lydia said.

Not really. He had a feeling most people didn't really know Wes. "A little bit." Questions swam in her eyes. He had no doubt one of them probably circled around his sexuality, and if he was gay or not. He didn't hide the fact that he liked to have a good time. He didn't hide the fact that he enjoyed men as well, but it wasn't part of his standard introduction.

He saw her confusion, though. Knew she'd probably seen him with women, probably pegging him for being in the closest. Bisexual wasn't something most people considered, or really believed, which, if you asked him, was bullshit.

"I'm going to go." With his thumb he pointed inside the room. "To find, Wes. I'll see you later." He bailed before she had the chance to ask questions.

The house wasn't huge, but he still couldn't find Wes. At least not in the obvious places. He said a quick hello to Cooper and Noah when someone tugged on his arm.

"Hi," Jessie said when he looked down at her.

"Hi."

"My polish is coming off."

"I'm sorry. I bet Uncle Wes would repaint it. I heard he's very good at nail polish."

Jessie's eyes sparkled with happiness. "Good." Jock snuck from the other side of him and licked the side of her face.

"Jock—" Jessie's giggle cut him off from saying anything

else.

"You brought him! Can we play? I wanna play!"

As if he could read her mind, Jock's tail started wagging like crazy.

"Well, I'm not sure. It's dark and cold outside, so I don't know if you're able to. Maybe we can ask Wes."

She crooked her finger at him, as if to say to come here. Braden kneeled next to her. "He's hiding."

Amusement pumped through him. "Is he?" From Braden or everyone in general, he wondered.

"Yep!" And then she ran off without him knowing where she went. The kid was a ball of energy; not that he could talk.

Noah and Cooper asked him about Jessie, and the dog. He just got through explaining that he'd seen them at the grocery store and she asked about Jock before Jessie returned, wearing a coat, gloves and a hat. "There's a flooding light in the back yard. Aunt Lydia said we could go out there."

He snickered at how she pronounced it. "Thank God for flooding lights." Braden stepped back. "Ladies first. Lead the way."

Jessie smiled and did exactly as he said, leading him to the backyard. They had a decent sized yard, with a wood fence and a swing in a tree.

He pulled the ball from his coat pocket and handed it to her. "Here you go."

Over and over she threw the ball for Jock, who happily ran to get it and bring it right back to her. Braden watched, teasing her and asking for a turn every once in a while. After he threw the ball once, Jock went after it and Jessie tugged on his hand again. "Do you like boys like Uncle Wes?"

He coughed, choking on something in his throat that wasn't there. Had he asked questions like this at her age? Holy shit. What was he supposed to say? This wasn't the kind of talk he wanted to have with someone else's child. Was it better to tell the truth and say he went for both or not? "What do you think?" he asked.

Jock ran in circles around them, wanting the attention.

She shrugged. "Don't know."

"Does it matter either way?"

"Nope. Mommy says Uncle Wes used to love Alexander, and that his love was just the same as everyone else's. Do you know Alexander? I don't. Mommy said Uncle Wes loved him like she loved my daddy."

The urge to ask questions climbed up his throat but he held it back. Interrogating a kid probably wasn't a real kosher thing for him to do. "Jock's getting bored. Do you want to throw the ball for him again, or do you want me to?" Jessie chose to throw the ball, and Braden couldn't stop himself from wondering who Alexander was, and if maybe the man caused part of the loneliness he saw in Wes.

***

Wes peeked inside Jessie's bedroom, but didn't see her. His pulse sped up a bit, but he told himself to calm down. She had to be around here somewhere.

"Lyd, have you seen Jessie?" he asked when he found his sister in the kitchen.

"She's out back playing with Braden and his dog." She looked jittery, and he knew she wanted to talk to him about Braden, but thankfully she held off.

"It's cold and dark. She shouldn't be outside." The last thing he wanted was for her to get sick again so soon.

Lydia grabbed his arm before he could walk away. "The floodlight is almost as bright as the sun. She's wearing her jacket and gloves. She's fine, Wes."

He took a deep breath, knowing she was right. Still, he finished his walk to the other side of the older kitchen and slipped open the back door, to hear Jessie laughing.

Braden swung his arm around in a circle. "You throw farther if you wind up!" Then he swung his arm forward, both Jessie and Jock looking for the ball that he still held in his hand. "I think it went all the way to the moon. Might take it a bit to fall back down."

Jock ran back toward him but Jessie looked up at the sky, waiting for the ball to come back down again.

"Where? Where?" Jessie screamed.

"It's coming. Wait for it," Braden replied to her. When she wasn't looking he tossed the ball into the air, and as it came back down he yelled, "There it is!"

Wes smiled as his niece jumped up and down, giddy excitement pouring off her. Braden was good with her. Better with Jessie than him. His chest got tight at the thought. Jesus, he just wanted to do right by the little girl. He wanted her to be happy, and he knew he needed to start playing a more active role in making that happen. He wondered how Braden could do it, how the man seemed to be so happy all the time, and wondered why he couldn't be.

"Hey. Getch'a ass down here and play with us," Braden called to him as Jessie said, "Ooh. You said a bad word!"

Braden's big eyes went even wider than usual. "Shit. I mean shoot."

Wes laughed, but for some reason still didn't move from his spot by the door.

"Come down here before I get myself in more trouble." He eyed Wes more seriously than before, and then nodded his head back a little, as if to say *come here*. "Play with us, Wes… unless you're afraid I'm going to show you up."

He crossed his arms and leaned against the doorframe. "At a game of catch?"

"He can frow to the moon!" She turned the "TH" sound into an "F" like she did sometimes. The excitement radiated off her, wrapping around Wes and pulling him out toward them. He wanted to make his niece happy like that. Chelle would have been able to do it. She tried to do it for him when they lost their mother.

"Nah, Braden has nothing on me. Let me see the ball."

"Big talker. Can you deliver?" Braden winked at him as he

tossed Wes the ball.

Wes caught it. "Wouldn't you like to know?" He was flirting with the man but didn't want to think about that. If he did, he'd stop. Right now he didn't want to stop. Right now he wanted to have fun. Wanted to forget the fact that he never really flirted with anyone. He picked guys up for an anonymous fuck once in a while, much like he'd done with Noah, but he didn't flirt. That meant you planned to see them again, and for years, Wes tried to avoid emotional ties.

Tonight wasn't about that, though.

"What do you think, Jess? Can I throw farther than Braden?"

Poor Jock ran around them, just wanting his damn ball back, as Jessie hugged Wes. She wrapped her little arms around his leg and said, "Hug for luck. You can do it."

His chest swelled at her belief in him. "Thanks, kiddo."

He pulled his arm back to throw but Braden's voice interrupted him. "You have to wind up first. It goes farther that way." He had a mischievous look on his face, raised brows and a cocky grin, as though to say he didn't think Wes would do it.

Well, he would have another thing coming.

"Watch out. I'm going to need space for this."

Happily, Jessie skipped a few feet away.

"You're going to regret that, Braden."

He cocked a brow. "Doubt it." Something about the smoothness of his voice, the way he took Wes in with his eyes, serious yet playful at the same time, told him Braden didn't mean he thought Wes wouldn't win their pretend contest. But maybe that he saw Wes needed to enjoy himself a little, and that Braden wanted to see it.

I'm going crazy. This man doesn't know me enough to care about that, and I don't know him enough for it to matter.

Wes ignored those thoughts. He'd gotten good at ignoring things. He spun his arm around the way Braden had done. He pretended to release the ball and said, "Did you see it, Jess? It went so fast I could hardly keep my eyes on it."

"Where? Where, Uncle Wes?"

He pointed. "It went way over there. I think it's still going."

"I think it went farther than mine."

Braden stepped closer to them, and Wes found himself replying in the most unusual way. "Yeah?"

Confusion tugged the corners of Braden's lips down. "Yeah." And then he pulled Jessie's attention away with, "Look over there. Is that it?" She faced away from him so Wes was able to throw the ball high into the air for it to fall back down in front of them.

Jessie looked up at him. "I bet it went all the way to Heaven and Mommy frew it back."

Threw, Wes almost corrected. The need to pull her close filled him. He wrapped an arm around her, needing her close. "Yeah. Yeah, I think so, kiddo."

Braden pushed his hands into his pockets, looking like he worried he shouldn't be here. Jock ran off with his ball, probably thankful to have it back, while Wes held his niece, wishing she hadn't lost her mom. Wishing they all hadn't lost her.

Chapter Seven

Braden lingered around the house as everyone started to clear out. Wes had gone into Jessie's room with her a little while ago to put her to sleep. Braden should probably leave too. The only people still here were himself, Lydia and her family, Cooper and Noah. The last time he lingered things hadn't gone well between them, but he still didn't walk toward the door and go.

"How's the rehab going?" he asked Cooper as he put on his coat.

"Good. I'll be back out there with ya before you know it." He couldn't hide the eagerness in his voice. Cooper was born to fight fire, just like Braden and every good firefighter was.

"Good. We need you out there."

"Don't tell him things like that. He already has a big enough head." Noah wrapped an arm around Cooper.

"Come on. You don't want to complain about that, do you?" Cooper elbowed Noah.

"Hell, do you guys ever stop? I swear, Bradshaw, you're asking for me to give you shit," he teased. The two men laughed before saying their goodbyes and leaving.

Lydia approached him next. "My kids are getting tired, so I think Stan and I are going to go. Would you mind telling Wes goodbye for us?"

He held back his chuckle. The sparkle in her eyes said she hoped to be giving them alone time together. "No problem."

She gathered up her clan to leave. Almost the second she had the door closed, Wes came out of Jessie's room.

"She asleep?" Braden asked.

"Yeah." His eyes scanned the living room.

"Everyone left. Your sister said to tell you goodbye, but I'm pretty sure she'd still be here if I wasn't. I think she was trying to leave us alone."

He wasn't sure if Wes would be annoyed by his comment, but

to Braden's amusement, he just said, "I see you know Lydia well. She's been doing this to me since she realized I would never hook up with her girlfriends."

Braden suddenly wished Wes had another tie on that he could hold him with. "What?" he nudged Wes's arm. "You mean I'm not special?"

Wes rolled his eyes. "Does that usually work for you?"

"Usually. I have a feeling you're going to prove me wrong, though." He hoped Wes wouldn't, but there was a small part of him who hoped he would. He liked that about Wes. He did what he wanted and said how he felt, and he didn't give Braden whatever he wanted, the way most people did.

"I just think it's a waste of breath. Even if I planned to fuck you again, it wouldn't be with Jessie in the other room." He could tell Wes wasn't trying to be a prick with his comment—just being honest, and worrying about his niece.

"I know. Doesn't mean it's not a whole hell of a lot of fun to see you fluster, though. I think you need the excitement of having Braden Roth as a friend. You have to admit, I keep things interesting, even if it is just by pissing you off half the time."

He expected Wes to end the conversation there, but instead he crossed his arms and said, "You flirt and try to fuck all your friends?"

"Nope. Just you." This time, Wes did pull back. The look in his eyes sobered, and he went toward the kitchen.

Yep, he screwed up again. Open mouth, insert foot. But then, from the other room, Wes asked him, "You want a beer?"

Braden exhaled a breath and realized he would have been upset if he'd fucked this up and had to leave. The fact was, he enjoyed being around Wes. Enjoyed shaking his life up a little. He liked the idea of being the man's friend. "Sure."

Wes emerged a few seconds later with two open bottles of Corona. "Come on," he nodded toward the front door. "Let's go outside."

Jock followed them as they went to Wes's mostly-enclosed front porch. It had a porch swing on one end, and two chairs close to the door. Between the chairs sat an outdoor heater, which Wes turned on.

"Can you just close the screen door? I want to hear Jessie if she gets up," he asked Braden.

"No problem."

Jock curled up next to the heater as the two men sat in chairs.

He doesn't want to be alone, Braden realized. Wes would never admit it, and hell, maybe he didn't know himself, but he didn't want to be alone.

Braden had never in his life known what it felt like to truly be alone. If he felt like being around someone, he called a friend up and made plans. He had a great family that he was close to. People who knew everything about him and accepted him for who he was. Wes had the family who loved him, but he had a feeling Wes struggled to accept it. Those thoughts made him sorry for the man.

"Thanks." Wes took a drink of his beer. "For bringing Jock and for playing with her out there. She had a blast with you."

Braden swallowed a mouthful of beer, feeling the warmth spread through him due to Wes's words. "Eh. It's just because I'm probably a bigger kid than she is." He turned Wes's way. "She had fun with you, too."

"I need to do that more often."

Did Wes not think he did enough? "Are you fucking kidding me? She's probably the happiest kid I've seen, and my siblings are working on a football team. I've been around a lot of kids. You're doing great, man. Especially considering everything that's happened."

Wes didn't turn to look at him, just stared through the opening in the porch, into the darkness.

"I built this porch for her. She was always cold, but it got worse when she got sick. She liked to sit outside but didn't want to always be in the back. She was crazy, used to watch the headlights on the cars that drove by and tried to decide where they were going." He paused but Braden didn't speak, knowing Wes would continue when he was ready. "I know it's random for a porch out here, but I built this so she could be outside but keep warm."

The pain in Wes's voice slammed into Braden's chest. But he felt something else, too—pride. He was honored and surprised that the man would share this with him.

"You put me to shame in the brother department."

Wes chuckled like Braden hoped he would. They were quiet after that, each taking drinks of their beer. It was Wes who spoke first. "Thanksgiving is in a month…and Christmas. How am I supposed to—" He shook his head. "Never mind."

"Hey." He realized it might be a mistake, but Braden reached over and sat his hand on Wes's arm. "I'm pretty good at keeping my mouth shut when I need to. You can talk to me." He brushed his thumb over Wes's arm, enjoying the feel of his heat, his muscles, the tickle of the hair there.

"No, I can't. It's not you, though. I don't talk to anyone." He pushed to his feet. "I'm going to grab another beer. You want one?"

Braden nodded, knowing that even though it wasn't much, Wes had just given him something.

***

Wes opened the fridge and grabbed two more beers. Really he just wanted a minute to himself, some space to hopefully make that suffocating feeling in his chest ease up. The holidays—he wasn't even sure where that thought had come from all of a sudden, or why he shared it with Braden. But the truth was, they did linger around the corner, and he had a little girl sleeping in the other room who he had to make them special for. Who he wanted to make them perfect for.

Another truth singed the edges of that thought. He'd never spent a Christmas with Jessie. He hadn't spent one with Chelle or Lydia in years. Work was always an excuse. They knew, though. Knew that he'd come to see them less and less, which pretty much made him a bastard.

Wes shook his head. Jesus, he'd been feeling sorry for himself a lot lately. Not just lately; years, it seemed.

After twisting off the lids to their beers, he tossed them into the trash before heading back to the porch. "Here you go." He handed the bottle to Braden and took the seat beside him.

"It's relaxing out here." Braden kicked his feet up and rested them on the railing.

"It is. Would be a nice place to paint."

Wes felt Braden's eyes on him, so he turned to face him and made himself grin. "What? That surprises you?"

"Nah. Totally used to you being a completely open book and sharing pieces of your life like that. You paint?"

He remembered Braden's words from the kitchen the other night, winked, and repeated what he said. "I'm a man of many talents."

Braden laughed. "Always bustin' my balls. You're lucky I like you. Especially when you're like this."

Wes almost asked him what he meant but realized he might already know. He wasn't even sure when the switch had flipped inside him, changing his mood. "You make it easy," he teased.

"Easy to bust my balls, or it's easy to be in a good mood around me?" He swallowed a mouthful of beer, looking at Wes over the bottle. The bastard. He had that cocky glint in his eyes, the mischievous curl to his lips. "I think you like me, too. One of these days you're going to admit it."

Wes rolled his eyes, realizing he tried to hold back a smile. "Don't hold your breath."

"Would you give me mouth-to-mouth?"

He couldn't fight it this time and let out a chuckle. "Now you're moving into cheesy territory. You should stop while you're ahead." But then, Wes wanted to hold onto the lightness around them, too. Wanted to cling to it for once in his life because it felt a whole lot better than the alternative.

He took another drink. "It'd probably be easier than getting rid of the body."

Braden let out a loud laugh. "Fucker. I'll remember that. I guess we should change the subject, then. I wouldn't want to get too cheesy on you and force you into mouth-to-mouth or digging a hole. When do you start work?"

A little sting of regret burned him at the subject change. "This week. I'm on Mondays, Tuesdays, and Wednesdays. I'm probably going to have to put Jess in daycare for a couple hours on Wednesdays, which I fucking hate. Lydia works a little later that day. I was hoping to get it off but it would screw up their rotation." It was another change for her. She'd never been in daycare her whole life. Chelle and Lydia had always been able to work their schedules so they could help each other out.

"Can I ask where her dad is?" Braden leaned forward, rubbing a hand on Jock's head before sitting back again.

"Died. She couldn't have been more than a few months old. Life is really fucked up sometimes. She's not even five and she's lost both her parents." He shook his head, set the bottle of beer down, then leaned forward. What was with their family and losing everyone who meant something to them? *Alexander may not have died but he walked away from Wes and never looked back.*

Wes tensed when he felt Braden's hand at the back of his neck. "I work Sunday, Monday and Tuesday."

Wes turned Braden's way, the man's rough hand still against his skin. "I can't ask you to do that."

"You didn't."

"You can't want to. That's a lot of responsibility every week."

"Are you kidding me? She's a blast. She just might be the only person who can keep up with me, anyway."

Braden brushed his finger through the hair at the nape of Wes's neck, and damned if desire didn't make Wes's cock start to rise.

"Say yes." Braden's voice went deep. "Don't overthink it, don't worry. I'll take a background check for you if you need me to. I want to help. Just say yes."

The word "no" sat uncomfortably on his tongue. They didn't need to intertwine their lives like this. Jessie was his responsibility. But then he thought about how much fun Jess had with Braden. He trusted her with him. He didn't know if that was the right thing. Would Chelle have trusted him?

He didn't know about her, but Wes did. "Yes," he said. Braden nodded. When Wes leaned back, Braden didn't move his hand. And Wes didn't tell him to.

"Did she ever watch the sun rise from out here?" Braden asked.

A smile suddenly pulled at his lips. "Yeah. Yeah, she did."

"When was the last time you watched the sun rise, man?"

Hell, he couldn't even remember. "I don't know."

"Then we'll do it. No excuses, no reason. We'll just do it because we can, and because we want to."

It didn't matter that he'd been tired earlier, or that they'd be sitting our here for more hours than he wanted to count. He wasn't sure he'd ever really *wanted* to watch the sun rise before, but suddenly it was important.

"Yeah…yeah, let's do it."

There were long periods of quiet, but also talking, too. Wes made coffee, and Braden let Jock out to stretch his legs once or twice.

When the sun peeked out from behind a mountain, pinks and oranges in the sky, he realized why Chelle would sometimes do this. Wished he would've done it with her. And glad he'd done it with Braden. No one else would have thought to do something like this.

"Jesus, that's fucking beautiful."

"Yeah it is," Braden replied, and then pushed to his feet. "Now you can say you spent the night with Braden Roth."

Wes looked up at him. "More like you can say you spent the night with me."

Braden winked. "Finally." He turned for the screen door on the porch. "Come on, Jock, let's go."

The dog got up and followed him, and Wes watched. Watched until Braden's truck drove out of sight.

Chapter Eight

Around five thirty, on the fourth Wednesday that Braden watched Jessie, his phone rang. He pulled it out of his pocket to see Wes's name light up on the screen. He grinned and said, "You're bringing us dinner, right? I'm exhausted, honey. I don't know if I can handle cooking tonight. I feel like you're never home anymore."

Wes briefly chuckled. "Funny."

"Made you laugh." He took it almost as a personal goal to make Wes laugh as much as he could. The man didn't do it nearly enough. And he *was* pretty good at it.

Wes didn't reply to his comment, and instead said, "We're crazy around here. We have a trauma ten minutes out. Anna's working the ER tonight but she's not feeling well. She said she could stay until seven when someone gets in to cover for her, but—"

"But you want to help." He already realized that's who Wes was. He'd do more for others than he'd do for himself. "It's cool. We got this. I'll order a pizza or something."

"Yay!" Jessie screamed and Braden ruffled her hair.

"Are you sure? Anna can stay if you have somewhere to go. Or I could call Lydia."

"It's cool. You'd feel guilty if you left her to work when she didn't feel well. I have your number, man. We can even pretend it was my idea and you didn't have to ask if you want."

Wes paused, which wasn't a surprise to Braden. He always seemed taken aback when Braden called him on something, when Braden called people on most things.

"I need to get to the ER. I…thanks."

"No problem. Go save lives. We'll be here when you get done." He hung up before Wes could. Braden stood up. "Uncle Wes is going to be a little late, so we're on our own for dinner tonight. What do you like on your pizza?"

Jessie grinned up at him. "Cheese."

"And?"

Her nose wrinkled, as though she didn't know what he meant.

"You only eat cheese on your pizza? You're missing out, Squirt. Do you trust me?"

Another confused look.

"Never mind. I got this. You're about to have the best pizza you've ever put in your mouth." Braden made the quick call to order their dinner. They had time to watch a couple episodes of *Tom and Jerry* before the doorbell rang.

After paying, he walked over to the coffee table but Jessie said, "We can't eat dinner in the living room. Mommy says it's good to eat dinner at the table."

Oh. "Cool. We can handle the table." Wes usually worked six a.m. to six p.m. Braden usually left not long after Wes got home, so he hadn't done the dinner thing with them except when Jessie was sick. He figured that didn't really count, though.

"What about the TV? You have to turn off the TV."

Oh. "Why do we have to turn off the TV?" He set the pizza boxes on the table. All three of them.

"Cuz dinner is to talk. Mommy says that's when you talk about your day."

Oh. And yeah, he was fully aware he'd thought *Oh* three times in a row, but often it felt like Jessie was the one watching him. Chelle must have been great. It made sense considering Jessie seemed smarter than any four-year-old he knew. "Sounds good to me." He gave them each a paper plate, thinking about the fact that Jessie spoke about her mom as though she was still around. "You have to try this: pepperoni, sausage, onion and black olives. I know it doesn't sound good, but it's great."

Jessie stuck her tongue out. "Ew. That's yucky."

"Yucky? It's the Braden special," he teased but she didn't look impressed. "Fine. I bought you a cheese pizza, too. Don't think I won't remember this, though."

"Why?"

"I don't know. Ignore me."

They finished eating. Braden cleaned up the mess afterward and Jessie watched him like she always did. "Are you having a sleepover?" she asked.

I wish, kid. "No. Your uncle will be home around seven thirty, so he'll put you to bed."

"How come you never have a sleepover? I sleep at Aunt Lydia's."

Hell. Why did he always get these questions? "Because I have my own house. I just like to hang out with you for a few hours on Wednesdays."

"Don't you want to sleep over? It would be fun."

Yes, yes he did. He very much wanted to spend the night with Wes again.

Braden put the milk in the fridge. "I'm sure it would be, but…it just doesn't work that way." How the hell did he put it other than that?

"Why?"

Braden really wished he could ban that word tonight. "I'm craving ice cream. How about you?"

That easily, her questions stopped and her eyes went big. He'd have to remember to make sure Wes always had ice cream in the house.

After they had their snack, Jessie curled up with Jock on the living room chair and watched TV. She yawned about eight hundred times, and he thought about putting her to bed, but he had no clue what he needed to do to get her ready. He glanced at his cell. It was already eight. Where the hell was Wes?

Just as he went to dial, the door opened and Wes came in. "Uncle Wes!" Jock and Jessie both jumped off the chair and ran to greet him.

Braden watched Wes's tired eyes brighten as he hugged the little girl. It didn't change the bags he had there, or the slump of his body. He was obviously tired as hell.

"We had pizza and ice cream!" Jessie told Wes, who looked at Braden over her head.

"Oh, did you?"

"Is that a bad thing?" Braden asked.

Wes shook his head. "Nah. It's okay to treat her sometimes." Even his voice sounded lower and more exhausted than usual.

Jessie yawned and Wes picked her up. "Let's get you to bed." He caught Braden's eyes. "Sorry I'm late. I—"

"Get her to sleep. I'll hang around and we can talk when you're done."

Wes nodded and disappeared down the hall. Damn, he respected the hell out of the man for everything he did. And he wished there was more he could do to help. It hadn't started this way, but he really did consider Wes a friend. He enjoyed his company, and for the first time in his life, outside of work, he was doing more than just going out to get laid or have fun. He felt like what he did mattered, even if it was just to a curly-haired little girl and her uncle, who Braden liked to see smile.

***

After Wes got Jessie into bed, he went to his room and changed out of his scrubs and into a pair of sweatpants and a shirt. His stomach growled and his bed called his name, but he knew that if he lay down, he wouldn't be able to sleep anyway. His mind didn't want to shut down lately, picking night to run wild.

When he made it back to the living room, Braden sat at the table in front of three pizza boxes. "Hungry?" he asked.

"Jessie wanted cheese. I didn't know what you liked, so I figured I'd be safe with pepperoni. And then I needed mine, too."

Wes opened one of the boxes and set a few pieces on a plate. "You didn't have to get a whole cheese pizza for her, or a whole one for me. Let me know how much it was and I'll pay you back."

"Nah. It's not a big deal."

Wes sighed. "Yes, it is."

"Then I guess you'll have to buy next time."

Wes wasn't in the mood to argue, so he went over and sat on the couch.

"I was told we aren't allowed to eat dinner in the living room. I might have to tell on you."

A laugh sat on the sidelines but he didn't have the energy to get it out. "Don't go getting me in trouble."

They were mostly quiet while Wes ate. He wondered why Braden stayed, but then realized he didn't mind the company and didn't mention it. When he finished eating he set the plate down and tossed a crust to Jock, who caught it. "I am so fucking tired." He dropped his head back and closed his eyes. "We lost the patient. It was a MVA. I always…" He sighed, knowing he wouldn't finish that statement. Motor vehicle accidents were tough for him, especially when they lost the patient. He always pictured his mom.

"Anyway, I ran a few minutes late from that, and then someone needed a ride home and they were a little out of the way. Sorry again for being late. I owe you one." He owed him more than that if he would admit it.

"Do you want me to go so you can get some sleep?"

Wes opened his eyes, rolling his head to the side so he could still lean back against the couch but could see Braden, too. He had his leg pulled up, his ankle resting on a knee. He had on a long-sleeved shirt, but like most of what he wore, it was pulled taut across the hard planes of his body. His dark hair looked like he'd run his hand through it over and over; Wes realized it pretty much always looked like that. He hadn't had his hands in that hair enough the night they spent together.

"I'm tired as hell but can't seem to relax enough to go to sleep. I toss and turn half the night." He shut up there and hoped Braden wouldn't ask why. Wouldn't pry into things Wes would rather not talk about.

And thankfully, Braden didn't ask. He just looked at Wes with an expression in his eyes that Wes didn't understand. No, that was a lie. He knew what it was. Lust.

Braden stood, walked over, and sat on the coffee table in front of him. Arguments and words teased his tongue but he didn't let any of them out, just continued to lean against the couch and look at Braden.

"When was the last time you've done anything for yourself? The last time someone has done something for you?" Braden didn't move closer as he waited for Wes to answer.

"Why? What does that have to do with anything?"

"You work extra hours when you're exhausted to help someone else out. You give someone a ride when we both know you just wanted to be home. And that's just what I know about from today. What do you do for you? What do you let someone else do for you?"

Plenty of people in his life had made sacrifices for him— Chelle, Lydia, his mom. "Don't try and make a hero out of me. And you watched my niece for me tonight. You watch her every week, so I could say the same thing to you. You do something for me every week."

Braden shook his head. "Nah. I don't do that for you. Jessie's cool to hang out with and you're nice to look at. I'm here for me."

The air in the room thickened. Wes's body began to overheat. He wanted to feel something, something besides worry and stress and fear.

And Braden was more than just nice to look at. He had a dimple below his mouth that Wes suddenly wanted to taste. Wanted to put his hand in the hair he'd been admiring and fist it tightly there.

"I want you." Braden pushed toward the edge of the table.

"I have nothing to give right now." *I never do...* When Alexander walked out on him, when he hadn't been enough, he'd decided he'd never try to be again.

"I'm not asking you for anything. Well, except for you to let me get on my knees and blow you." He went down to the floor between Wes's legs and reached for his sweats.

Wes's hand shot out, wrapping around Braden's wrist. "Not here." His voice sounded gravelly, even to his own ears. "Not where Jessie could come out." Because no wasn't even a possibility. How could he turn this down? Braden had fucked him before. He'd almost been with Noah. Sex was just sex, and he was tired of fighting it. It had been different when Chelle was still alive. Different right after. But damned if he didn't need this right now.

"Hell yes." Braden stood and Wes was right behind him. He followed Braden to his bedroom, closing and locking the door behind them. As soon as the lock clicked into place, Braden went back to his knees again. "Jesus, it's been killing me not to have my mouth on you."

He put his forearm against Wes's stomach and pushed him backward, against the door. "I didn't get to suck your cock last time. I'm warning you right now, I'm good at this." He looked up at Wes and winked.

Wes shook his head but his lips still pulled into a smile. He grabbed a hold of Braden's dark hair and tightened his fingers in it. "You're the only man I know who still talks shit when he's about to have sex."

"Then you've been with the wrong kind of men."

"Prove it."

With eager hands, Braden shoved Wes's sweats down his legs. His dick ached as it sprung free, wanting nothing but the heat of Braden's mouth to envelope it. But he didn't take him deep right away. Braden's tongue started at the base of his erection, right above his balls, before he dragged his mouth upward, not stopping until his tongue circled Wes's head.

"Fuck." Wes squeezed his hand tighter in Braden's hair.

"I love the taste of cock." Braden licked his shaft again. "The hardness against my tongue but that soft, tender skin as well." He sucked Wes's balls into his mouth. "The saltiness of not just your flesh, but the reward I get, too." He tongued Wes's hole and the pre-come there. He buried his face in Wes's crotch. "The scent and the feel of rough hair against my face."

His cock jerked, and Braden snickered. The deep burn and tingle already pulled at him. "Then do it. Suck me," Wes gritted out.

"Why don't you make me?" Braden leisurely licked up his shaft again. "And don't go easy on me. It just pisses me off."

Wes didn't need another prompt. Braden opened his mouth and Wes thrust forward. He didn't shove his way completely into Braden's mouth, but *fuck,* if he didn't need to.

Braden sucked him, letting Wes control the pace, pumping in and out as he pleased. Soon Braden's hands were there, grabbing his ass and pushing, taking more of Wes's aching, hungry dick into his throat.

The need to come tied him in knots, but he wanted this to fucking last, too. He pulled out and Braden took the hint, lavishing his sac with more attention—licks, sucks, and then just shoving his face close and inhaling. Wes fucking loved that inhale.

Braden's voice was scratchy, full of sex when he said, "Spread your legs."

Wes did, and then Braden's hands were gone. He spit on one of his fingers before he found Wes's asshole. "I wish I could see that tight ring of yours, but I don't want to lose this, either." With that he took Wes's cock deep again, sucking him off. His finger rubbed Wes's hole. Each time he brushed over it, a tremor shook Wes's insides.

"Jerk me off, and push you finger inside me, too—fuck yes,"

he groaned when Braden fingered his hole. Braden's other hand worked with his mouth, making Wes's dick beg to explode.

That deep burn and tingle shot toward the surface, making it harder and harder for Wes to hold it off. When Braden's finger shoved deeper, rubbed against his prostate, he couldn't have held off if he wanted to. The orgasm bulldozed him as pulse after pulse filled Braden's mouth. He didn't stop sucking, or fingering, and Wes shot again before his whole body went limp like a noodle. Well, everything except his cock, that was still half-hard despite the monster orgasm. Wes let the door hold him up, deep breaths making his chest heave in and out.

"God, I love sucking dick," Braden said.

"And you proved you are really fucking good at it." Suddenly, he wanted his mouth on Braden, too. Wanted to feel the man's rod against his tongue.

"We have to be quiet and you can't stay long." He grabbed Braden and pulled him to his feet, but Braden shook his head.

"I have a hand that works just fine. Tonight was just for you. Relax. Get some sleep. You deserve it."

Stay lingered on his tongue but he didn't let the word free, for the first time easily accepting the gift that was given to him. Braden nodded his head to the side, telling Wes to move from in front of the door. He did, but when Braden's hand wrapped around the knob, Wes grabbed him, pulled Braden to him, and owned his mouth. He tasted himself on Braden's tongue as he sucked it, as he explored every part of his mouth before pulling away.

Braden smiled. "Good night. And have I told you I like this?" He fingered the hair on Wes's chin but didn't wait for a reply.

Braden got the door pulled open before Wes said, "Happy Thanksgiving…For tomorrow." It was a random comment, but he'd needed to say something.

Braden nodded. "You'll do great. You guys will have a good time. Get some sleep. I'll lock up."

And then Braden Roth was gone.

Chapter Nine

Braden had to leave his house at eight thirty the next morning to make it to his parents' place by ten. They wouldn't eat Thanksgiving dinner until about three, but he didn't make it home as often as he should, so when he did go, he went early.

He climbed out of his truck, taking in the two acres of land around the place he'd grown up. Living in Blackcreek was the closest he'd lived to their house since he left it at eighteen.

Not because he wanted away from them, or not because they weren't close, but there was a whole lot of world out there to see. But it was still beautiful out here. He'd always remembered how gorgeous it was every time he came home.

Braden pushed open the heavy, wooden door to the house his

parents had designed and built just as his mom walked by. Her blue eyes lit up. "Look who it is! My favorite son decided to come see me!"

She wrapped her thin arms around him, and Braden hugged her back as his brother Evan said, "Nice, Mom."

Evan smiled at Braden and embraced him when he parted from their mom. "She can't help it that she's smart." He patted Evan on the back. The truth was, Evan and their mom were very close...and exactly alike. "Are you two going at it again?" Braden asked.

"Yeah. I forgot she's always right." Evan rolled his eyes at their mom, Emmy, who hugged him.

"Oh, my boy is back. I missed my favorite son."

"Hey!" Braden pretended to try and pull them apart before the three of them started laughing.

After that, his mom made her way to the kitchen and Braden and Evan went to the living room, where his dad, two sisters, their husbands, Evan's wife, and six nieces and nephews ran around. Football blasted through the TV because his dad's hearing was going a little, even though he'd never admit it.

"Uncle Braden! Uncle Braden!" A whole herd of kids from

age eleven down came at him.

"Did you bring me a fireman sticker?" his nephew Tommy asked, and Braden pulled a few out of his pocket and handed them to him.

He went down the line, talking to and hugging all of them, before he walked over to his sister, Yvonne, to say hello. Her belly looked like someone stuffed a basketball into it, another new baby planning to make an appearance soon.

"Good to see you, baby brother." His other sister Lizzy grinned at him. They all spoke for a few minutes before he went over and sat next to his father to shoot the shit with him for a few minutes, too. Man, it felt good to be home.

"Hey, old man." Braden put a hand down on his dad's shoulder. Where Evan and his mom had a similar personality, Braden and his dad did, too. Though he guessed in a way he shared a lot of traits with his mom as well, but he and his dad had the same hair and eyes. The same strong build, and they both liked to laugh.

"Do I have to kick your ass to show you I still got it? Wouldn't want to embarrass you in front of the family."

"What if you break a hip?"

"What? Break a hip? You better take that back." He stood up to pretend to go after Braden, but in the end just squeezed Braden's shoulder the way Braden had just done with him. "Come on. I got something to show you."

Braden followed his dad outside and to the workshop he, his dad and Evan built when Braden was twelve. When they made their way inside, his eyes landed on an old Harley. He could have came right there. "Holy fuck. She's beautiful. Does Mom know?"

His dad laughed. "Of course she knows. I'm not stupid enough to lie to her about it. She likes to pretend it doesn't exist, though, so she's made me promise not to even talk to her about it. It needs a little work, which gives me something to do. Who would have thought retirement would be so damn boring? I'm going crazy."

Yeah, Braden could imagine he'd be the same way. "Damn." He ran his hand over the chrome handlebars. "I wish she was ready right now. I'd love to ride her."

"You get four days off in a row every week. Come down and spend a few of them with me and we'll work on her." His father walked to the fridge he kept in the shop and pulled out a beer for each of them, handing Braden one.

He twisted the lid and took a drink. "Maybe I can figure

something out. I'm helping a friend of mine out, though. He just got custody of his niece and I watch her for him sometimes."

"How'd he get custody?" Dad asked.

Braden picked at his beer. "Lost his sister to cancer. It's been tough on him."

"That's hard."

Yeah, yeah it was. "They'll be okay, though. Wes has his shit together."

Over the bottle, his dad's eyebrows rose. "Is this just a *friend* or a *special friend?*"

Braden almost snorted Coors Light. His family all knew he was bi, and it shouldn't shock him that his dad would come out and say something like that. "Christ, Dad, please don't ever say 'special friend' to me again. He's just a buddy who has had some hard times, and I like helping him out. He's a good guy. You'd like him. And Jessie is cool as hell. She'd have a blast with the army they're building in the house."

His father's brows drew together and Braden found himself adding, "He's a friend."

Again his dad put a hand on his shoulder and squeezed. "Just don't look your mother in the eyes if you say that to her, okay? She's already stressing about when her youngest is finally going to settle down, and something tells me she wouldn't believe what you're saying to me."

What could he say to that? That he'd fucked Wes before? That he wouldn't mind doing it again? Besides friendship, that's all they had between them and as close as he was with his family, he didn't talk to them about his sex life.

He and his dad screwed around with the motorcycle a little before Braden went inside to help his mom cook. By the time they all sat around the table, his gut hurt from how much he'd laughed today. But not enough to slow him down on the food. They talked and he fielded questions about his love life and teased his siblings about all the damn kids.

"Are you going to stay here tonight?" his mom asked as the whole family helped clear the table. Yvonne and her family would be, but Evan and Lizzy both lived within a mile or so. "We can make a big breakfast in the morning."

"Stay, Uncle Braden!" one of his nieces shouted.

He shrugged. "Yeah, I probably will." He'd missed being around his whole family and wasn't ready to go yet. Still, watching them all, he couldn't help but wonder about Wes and Jessie, hoping their day was as good as his.

***

Wes's gut ached as he watched Jessie push her food around on her plate. She hadn't been herself all day. Little periods of the smiling, happy girl showed, but the clouds always lingered nearby.

He hadn't been sure how the holidays would go. He'd been worried, but there was also that hope that her age would help. That her still being so young would make things easier on her. But he'd seen the sadness in her eyes all day. She missed her mom. She knew today was a special day, and though she didn't totally grasp what it was, she knew they were spending the day with people they loved and her mother wasn't here.

His phone buzzed against his leg. Wes almost ignored it but then pulled the phone from his pocket to see a text from Braden.

How's it going over there?

Could be better.

Shit, man. I'm sorry.

Yeah, he was, too.

Not your fault.

Wes set his phone in his lap. "What's your favorite part of Thanksgiving dinner, Jess? Mine is the potatoes. I think I could live off mashed potatoes."

"Pie," she answered, giving him a brief smile.

"Hey. That's cheating. I didn't know dessert counted." He hoped his voice sounded lighter than the heaviness weighing him down.

"I miss Mommy." Jessie let her spoon fall to her plate and crossed her arms. Wes looked at Lydia, her husband, hoping one of them had the answer for him, then decided to do the best he could on his own.

"Come here, kiddo." He shoved his cell into his pocket as he walked over to her. Jessie wrapped her arms around his neck as he carried her out of Lydia's dining room. He rubbed the back of her head as she buried her face in his neck and cried.

"I know. I miss her, too." He took her to the room she slept in when she spent the night, and sat with her on the twin bed. "It's okay to miss her. You know she never wanted to leave you. You were her favorite person in the world. If she could be with you, she would be."

The whole time he spoke, the same sentences played in his head: Please let me be saying the right thing. Please let me do right by her.

"When will she come back?"

His heart broke, pain splintering him apart. "She won't come back, kiddo. Remember we talked about this."

"Why can't she come back?" Jessie cried harder.

I don't know. Sometimes he felt that the more people loved someone, the more guarantee they had of losing them. "Because she can't." How the hell did he explain this to her? How did he make her understand? "Remember how we talked about this? That when people die, it's almost like they're asleep and can't wake up?"

Jessie nodded.

"She loved you so much. And we need to remember her all the time. It's good to think about her and talk about her. Remember how you said you like pie the best? Your mommy did, too."

Jessie giggled.

"When I was a little boy, she hid a fake spider in my pie once and I cried."

She laughed even more at that. "You were a little boy?"

"What?" Wes ruffled her hair. "I'm going to pretend you didn't say that."

He held her for a few more minutes, and when she calmed down, they went back to finish dinner with the family. Jessie talked more, but he could still tell she was sad, confused.

After dinner they played Go Fish and Uno, him and Jessie on the same team. When the kids were tired, they decided to watch TV. "I'm going to clean up some of the mess in the kitchen, Lyd."

She shushed him. "You don't need to do that."

Yes I do. She must have seen it in his eyes because she didn't say anything else as Wes disappeared into the kitchen, needing to be alone. It didn't take much time for him to load the dishwasher, but the antsy, heavy feeling taking him over hadn't subsided at all. He shook his hands out, leaned on the counter with his head in his hands, and took a few deep breaths.

You'd think after all this time he would be used to losing people.

And then he did the strangest thing. It was as if his hand acted on its own, with no command from his brain. He pulled out his cell and texted Braden.

She asked me why her mom can't come back. How the

fuck do I make her understand when I'm so pissed off about it myself?

The second he hit send, he typed out another reply.

Don't call.

It was a whole hell of a lot easier to type than talk.

I would have called.

I know

It made his stomach uneasy that he knew that.

Death is hard for any of us to understand. All you can do is love her.

It didn't feel like enough.

Sorry. I'm sure you're busy with your family.

What the fuck was wrong with him? Why did he text Braden to ruin his Thanksgiving, too?

Don't be sorry.

Wes didn't reply, and then another text came from Braden.

I have a black eye.

Wes flipped the phone around in his hand a few times, almost going back into the living room, but he had to ask.

How the hell did you do that?

Got beat up by a two year old ;)

Wes chuckled. The man was fucking crazy.

I put up a good fight, though.

Not good enough, obviously.

For a few more minutes they texted back and forth. Wes wasn't stupid. He knew Braden just wanted to distract him, and damn it, he wanted that, too. Deciding he'd hid in the kitchen enough, Wes told Braden he had to go. Braden replied to have a good night and that he was staying out with his parents that night.

Happy Thanksgiving, Wes told him, before putting his phone away.

Three hours later he sat on the front porch of his house, looking out at the night, when his cell buzzed again. Without looking, he knew it was Braden. Sure enough, the message on the screen said,

How you doing?

Lonely. Scared. Angry. **Okay. Jess stayed at Lydia's tonight. Thought it would be good for her to be around the kids.**

What are you doing?

Sitting on the porch

It was about five minutes before Braden replied.

Watch the headlights of the next vehicle that passes and try to guess where they're going.

Wes looked out to the street, saw the two white globes slow down in front of his house, and he knew. He fucking knew it was Braden.

He didn't let himself think about the why of him being here, or that he'd gladly let him in. Wes just replied,

Here.

And then waited for Braden to turn down his driveway.

Chapter Ten

Braden opened the screen door on Wes's porch. Once they'd started texting, he couldn't get the man out of his mind. He'd taken a shower to try and relax, and the second he got out, he knew he'd come—because he wanted Wes, wanted to help him forget like he had the night Wes had gone with him from the bar. He had this need to do something important for Wes. Not that he was selfless or anything, because just as much as those other things, he just plain wanted Wes.

There was more to it even than that, though. He didn't want Wes to be alone. The man would never ask for help, wouldn't ask for someone to be there, but Braden wanted to make sure Wes knew he would be. He hated to think about anyone feeling completely alone in the world, but...*fuck*, it gutted him to think of

Wes feeling that way.

They faced off, nothing but hard stares, cold air and tension between them.

"Why are you here?" There was a roughness to Wes's voice, tiredness wrapped around confusion. He held the same look in his eyes, but that wasn't the only thing there. Desired flared in his almond-shaped eyes that Braden had no doubt Wes saw reflected in his own.

Still he said, "I'm here for whatever you need." Because that was true, too. Even if he knew there wouldn't ever be a chance to fuck Wes again, he'd be here.

As always, words seemed out of Wes's reach. Instead of trying to find them, he grabbed Braden by the collar of his jacket and pulled, the same way Braden had done with his tie. Finally he muttered, "I want to fuck you. I want to forget about everything else in my life and just focus on what I can control. Getting you hard." He cupped Braden's already hardening cock through his jeans. "Driving you wild... Tasting you everywhere."

His hand slid around behind Braden to palm his ass. "You said you love sucking dick but this is what I want right here. I want to lose myself in nothing but pleasure because right now I really fucking need something that just feels *good.*"

Braden's breath pushed out in a rush, like it participated in a race. Need, want and lust combusted together to light the deadliest of fires, and he wanted nothing more than to let it burn him alive.

"What's taking you so long? Show me what you can do."

The night they'd been together had been rushed and sloppy, but this…tonight he knew would be different, and he couldn't fucking wait.

Like that night months ago, Wes's mouth came down on Braden's first. It was just as rushed as their kiss on their first night, but not nearly as sloppy. Wes's tongue stroked his. He pulled back, his teeth digging slightly into Braden's bottom lip and giving it a pull.

"You bit me that first night."

Wes grinned, one of the most relaxed smiles Braden had seen from him, and said, "I'll bite you again tonight."

"Yet, we're still standing on this porch right now. I'm beginning to think you're all talk."

"You're the one who likes to talk. Not me."

Braden laughed, following Wes into the house. If he remembered correctly, Wes was a vocal lover. He might not use many words at other times, but he did when he fucked.

Door closed, lights out, they stumbled into Wes's small room together. There was hardly enough space for them to walk around the bed in the middle.

The bed was all they needed.

They each kicked out of their shoes, pulled off their clothes with hurried hands. His body thrummed with desire, eager and so damned ready to come.

Wes's hand, slightly sweaty and rough, touched his chest before sliding down over each rib, each plane of his stomach muscles, palmed his balls and then moved back up to wrap around Braden's shaft.

Braden thrust into Wes's palm before taking his mouth. He pushed his tongue past Wes's lips, moving along with each jerk of Wes's hand. Wes's movements sped up. His thumb brushed over Braden's head, rubbing the precome there.

The more he jerked Braden off, the deeper Braden kissed. His muscles started to tense but he fought it off. Wes chuckled against his lips, obviously knowing how close he already had Braden to the edge. At the last minute, his hand stilled.

It was at that moment that Braden realized what Wes was

doing. He said he wanted something he could control, and that's exactly what he intended to do. Everything else in his life was so up in the air, but this he ran the pace of. He wanted to decide when and how Braden came. He wanted to pleasure him because it was something he could give.

Braden was just the lucky motherfucker who got to be on the receiving end of it.

He backed away, climbed on the bed, laid on his back with his hands behind his head. "Are you going to start driving me wild now?"

His whole body buzzed when Wes laughed.

"Always so damned sarcastic."

"I keep things fun."

Wes's smile slid off his face, his eyes studying. Just as quickly as the look appeared on his face it was gone, and Braden's mind turned to mush as Wes's sexy, muscular body came toward him. As his mouth lowered over Braden's dick, sucking in as much as he could.

"Holy. Fucking. Hell. Yes. Fuck. Just like that."

Up and down, Wes blew him, taking him deep. On reflex,

Braden's body started to take over. His orgasm begging to be let loose as he fisted a hand in Wes's hair. As soon as he did, Wes pulled back.

"I want your mouth. You're driving me fucking crazy," Braden moaned.

"That's the point, remember?"

He got Wes's mouth again, except this time it was in a kiss. His lithe body ran the length of Braden's as he thrust their shafts together. That deep ache built inside him again as Wes's tongue went deep, as the hard planes of their bodies fit together.

There was nothing like the feel of another cock against his. The hardness as they rubbed one another. Braden reached between them, wrapping a fist around them both. His fingers didn't meet and it was a sloppy hold, but it got the job done.

Wes hissed as they kept thrusting, body against body. Dick against dick.

His fingers dug into Wes's arm when he yet again pulled back. "I want to come."

"You will." Wes jerked away, flipped Braden over so he lay on his stomach. "Hold it off, Braden. I want to fuck you till you come. Like I said earlier, you love sucking cock, but this right here is what I love."

Braden automatically spread his legs as Wes moved between them. "I want your ass."

Braden shuddered—actually *fucking shuddered,* experiencing this side of Wes. "Then take it."

"I didn't notice this before." He fingered the phoenix tattoo on Braden's upper back. "I like it."

"Admire it later. You want my ass, remember?"

Heat ripped down his spine at the feel of Wes's hands on his ass cheeks as he spread them wide. He was pretty sure the whole fucking world exploded when Wes's tongue traced his crack, *finally* landing on his hole.

***

Wes's mind transformed into a clean canvas, none of the chaos and angry colors that painted it before. In this moment, all he had on his mind was the task at hand—pleasure. To dish it out, and receive it. It was all he thought about, or felt.

And right now, he felt like doing nothing except eating Braden's ass.

"Spread your legs wider," he told him as he parted Braden's

cheeks again, burying his face between them.

Wes flicked his tongue rapidly back and forth over Braden's ring. Grunts and moans filled the air around them as Braden started to thrust his hips as though fucking the bed.

The man was on edge already. Wes could hear it in the sounds pulled from the back of his throat. From the jerking movements of Braden's body. And he fucking loved it.

He wanted to give Braden more.

He pulled his head back, sucking on his finger before pressing it where his tongue had just been. And then he pushed it inside, bit his teeth into Braden's right cheek as he did so, flying at the muttered, "Holy fuck" that passed Braden's lips.

He added his tongue to the mix, finger-fucking him but licking at his ring, too. He really loved nothing more than this, this licking and eating and savoring this part of a person that so many people found forbidden but to him was fucking incredible.

Braden's skin smelled like soap, but sweat and sex tinged the air too. It felt like a mask, a fog to block the rest of his life off from him for a limited amount of time.

He pushed another finger in, leaned up and watched as his fingers slid in and out. Braden's cheeks clinched, his thick, muscular, hairy thighs reminding Wes everything he loved about a man. "You're too damned sexy. Keeping my dick in my pants would be a whole lot easier if you weren't."

Which was true. Now really wasn't the time to…what? Have a new fuck buddy?

His circumstances tried to push their way in again, but then Braden spoke. "Your dick in your pants is the last thing either of us wants right now. Let it go. Enjoy it and put your goddamned tongue on me again. Neither of us thinks this means we're moving in together. There's nothing wrong with taking something for yourself."

He intended to do just that, though… "So this isn't for you, too?" He pushed his fingers deeper, hooked them and briefly brushed Braden's prostate before pulling them free and tonging him again.

"Fuck. This is so fucking for me."

Braden's ass moved against his mouth. He could do this all day, but his dick hurt, too, felt like it would explode if he didn't find himself inside Braden right fucking now.

Wes pulled back, got off the bed, and went to his closest. He had a box on the top shelf that he reached for.

"Nice view," he heard Braden say behind him, but he didn't reply. Just grabbed the lube and a condom, covering himself as he made it back to the bed in about two short steps.

Braden still lay on his stomach, his hands holding onto Wes's black headboard. Wes flipped open the lube, squirted a little on his dick and some in his hand before dropping it to the floor.

The second he lay on top of Braden, he spread his cheeks, lubed his hole and pushed inside. "Goddamn." He held himself still for a second so he didn't fill the condom right then. He pulled out before thrusting again.

His hands covered Braden's, and he held on. The hair on their arms and legs rubbed together. His ass fit against Wes's crotch as he worked him.

"Can you come like this? Do you need to be jerked off, too?" he asked.

Braden's reply was breathless. "If you fuck me hard enough."

Gauntlet thrown, challenge accepted.

He gripped Braden's hands tighter, pulled almost all the way out, then slammed forward again. Over and over he pumped into Braden, fucked him deep. "God, I love ass. You are so fucking tight."

Each time he pushed into Braden, the man's body thrust forward. Did he like the feel of the blanket rubbing against his cock? Like the slap of their bodies hitting together over and over again?

"Yeah…fuck. Right there," Braden gritted out. "Harder."

Wes pulled almost all the way out again and slammed forward. Their bodies slapped together again and he kept going. Faster, harder, until his orgasm was right fucking there.

While Wes pummeled him, he bit into Braden's shoulder at the same time, felt his body tense and shudder as he called out in completion, too.

"Holy shit." Wes rolled off him. "I needed to come."

Braden turned to his back, semen on his stomach. "You? I just sucked you off last night."

"You did? I don't remember." Wes's playfulness made his brows pull together. He wasn't usually like this after sex.

"If I could move I'd blacken your eye so it matches mine for talking shit, or do it again just so you could hear yourself scream again to remind you."

Wes shook his head, glancing at Braden's slightly darkened

eye. "I didn't scream." He pulled the condom off and tossed it into the trash, then grabbed a towel and wiped himself off. When he rolled back over, his body came into contact with Braden's. Braden, who looked thoroughly fucked and like he didn't plan on moving for a long time.

It made him proud.

It scared him to death.

Chapter Eleven

Braden felt the air in the room thicken. Or more correctly, he saw Wes's body stiffen—and not his cock, either. That he could handle.

"You never spend the whole night with anyone, do you?" He wasn't sure how he knew that's what had Wes freaked out right now, but he did. Because of Alexander, maybe? "Just curious, ya know. No one's ever left my bed before."

The air lightened when Wes shook his head. "You're so damn crazy." He paused a minute before adding, "No."

"That's a load off. I thought I was losing my touch." Braden reached over and rubbed his hand through the hair on Wes's stomach, leading to his cock. He liked to touch. Always had, and

Wes would have to deal with it.

"I don't think it's possible for you to even consider an option like that."

Wes had him there. "You're right. It's pretty impossible." He ran his finger over Wes's soft dick, down one thigh and up the other…just touching.

"You're going to get me hard again," Wes said.

"That a bad thing?" When Wes didn't answer, he said, "I love exploring someone else's body. I can tell when your breathing picks up, where you like to be touched. Feel little scars on your skin and I know a story lives in them. Don't know why." He leaned forward and licked Wes's nipple. "I find that sexy as hell."

Wes reached over, grabbing Braden's head and tilting it up so Braden could look at him. Damn it. He wanted to play again, but he had a feeling Wes wouldn't let him.

"This can't be something serious. Jessie is all that matters right now."

Braden pulled his head out of Wes's hold and bit Wes's finger. "I like to bite, too. And if you're being real, be completely real. I know Jessie is all that matters, but don't pretend that's the only reason you don't get serious. And I didn't ask you to be serious, anyway. We're friends. We're attracted to each other. We like spending time together. We like fucking every once in a while. In what world is that not the perfect kind of relationship there is? Friends with benefits, except I hate that saying. Friends who fuck? Friends who respect each other and like to get it on? Banging the babysitter?"

He knew he'd gone too far when Wes stiffened again.

Open mouth, insert foot.

"I'm kidding. I have a big mouth. Put your dick in it so I stop talking."

Unfortunately for Braden, Wes didn't listen. "She likes you. She's lost too much already. This can't affect her in any way, or it stops right now. Jessie comes first."

Braden leaned up so he could look Wes in the eyes, so the man could see how serious he was. "First of all, I want you to know I get it. She's a great kid and I would never hurt her. We're grown men. We like sex. We like sex together. To her I'll just be the guy her uncle is friends with, and who watches her once a week. It's not like either of us are looking for anything more than that, so it's all good. And second…those words that just came out of your mouth? Fucking remember them. When you feel like you're not doing a good job or you're upset because you don't think you're what she needs, remember what you just said. Remember how you always put her first. Remember that you would sacrifice anything for her. And remember that Chelle knew that, which is why she wanted you to have her. I respect the hell out of you, man. I want you to know that."

Wes visibly bit down. His eyes held Braden in a way that they never had. Not with anger or annoyance or even desire. Maybe gratitude; and a little bit of respect, too. It hit Braden right in the chest, little twitches of something he had never felt before coming to life where it touched. The crazy thing was, though he knew he could handle what he'd just told Braden—that they would just be friends who respect each other but also like to fuck—he thought he might be willing to try more with the man, too.

"Can we shut up now so I can suck your dick before I go?"

Wes nodded, gave him a half smile. "As normal, you're the one talking, not me."

He was right, so Braden stopped talking, leaned over Wes and sucked him deep. Cock in his mouth was much better than a foot.

***

Wes listened to the deep-rooted gurgle in the woman's lungs. "We're going to give you another breathing treatment, okay?" She nodded, used to the routine. She'd been living with COPD too long not to know the drill.

He confirmed her name while he set up the nebulizer, before opening the albuterol and filling it. Once he had everything set up, he held the mouthpiece out to her, but her hands shook too much for her to hold it.

"I'll do it for you, Mrs. Johnson."

The woman opened her wrinkled mouth before closing it around the mouthpiece and taking deep breaths. Wes held it there until the treatment ended, listened to her lungs again, which sounded much more clear, but not how healthy lungs would sound.

He finished putting things away, made some notes, told her to have a good day, and then left the room. Each footstep he took was heavy, knowing the older woman's breathing wasn't getting better. It was getting worse.

Wes clocked out, washed up, and then changed, putting the paper booties back on until he left the hospital. It hadn't been something he worried about before. Hell, he used to go home in his scrubs. But just recently he started thinking about the fact that there were too many fucking germs to take home to Jessie. It was one of the downfalls of his job.

After tossing the covers for his shoes in an outside trashcan, he went straight for his vehicle. Being Wednesday, that meant

Braden would have picked Jessie up from school and taken her home, so he didn't have to grab her up at Lydia's.

Just as his stomach growled, his phone rang. Braden lit up the screen. He hit talk. "Hey. Everything okay?"

"The Squirt is apparently dying of hunger. It just might kill her if she has to wait for you. She told me. And according to her, you'll be pissed at me if I let her starve."

"You said a bad word, Braden!" Jessie screeched in the background.

"Pissed is a bad word?" Braden asked.

"You said it again!"

"I was confirming!"

Wes's car swerved a little he was laughing so hard. "Okay, kids, time to stop fighting," Wes told them. Sometimes he wondered how the man could be almost thirty years old and still act like a kid. But then he went and said things like what he had the other night, for Wes to remember that Chelle wanted him to have Jessie, and he thought Braden had his shit together more than Wes did.

"Can I feed her? It will save you some time so you don't have to stop and she's right, I really don't want to risk pissing you off."

"Braden!" Jessie screamed.

Before they could get into it again, Wes interrupted, "If you want to, feel free. It's not a big deal for me to stop though." It's not like the man didn't do way more for Wes than he should.

"Nah, I got it. I'll make you guys something. Be careful. The weather's shitty out there."

Wes wasn't sure why that made him pause a second. "Yeah...yeah, I will. Thanks." It was cool of Braden to say that.

He hung up the phone, grateful that Braden decided to cook because he did pick something up most Wednesdays. It was much easier than cooking so late, and he wasn't the best cook, anyway.

The rest of the drive home went fairly quickly. When he walked in, Jock came running at him, his nose landing right in Wes's crotch. "Good to see you, too." He playfully pushed the dog's head away before Jock ran back over and laid on the floor under the table, probably waiting for Jessie to drop food for him.

The scent of bacon hit him, both Braden and Jessie turning to look at him. "Hey." He gave Braden a quick glance and the bastard winked at him. Wes rolled his eyes before planting a kiss on Jessie's forehead. "What ya eating?"

"BTL's."

"BLT's?" Wes confirmed.

"That's what I said, silly."

"Of course you did."

"There's food in the kitchen for you. All the stuffs there, you just gotta make your plate," Braden told him before taking another bite of his food.

"Thanks." Wes went into the kitchen and made his food. A few times, he glanced over his shoulder, to watch Braden and Jessie interact. She always laughed when Braden was around, laughed or scolded him for cursing, which was pretty hilarious when he thought about it.

Conflicting emotions tried to jerk him in too many different directions. No matter how much he tried, he couldn't cut off thoughts of the other night. Like Braden and he talked about. It was just sex. He could handle sex. But what would he do if they somehow caused problems for Jess? If he screwed it up like he often did, and Jessie lost someone who'd quickly become important to her? He wasn't sure he could risk that.

Wes gave them another quick glance as he finished making his sandwich. Jessie threw a Cheetos at Braden, and damned if the man didn't open his mouth and catch it.

"That's not fair!" Jessie crossed her arms before Braden ruffled her curls.

"Want me to teach you how to do it?"

Of course she said yes, and of course Braden tossed Cheetos at her, trying to land them in her mouth. When Jessie missed, Jock didn't.

Wes turned, leaning against the counter, and ate as he watched them play. No, he wouldn't let something screw this up. Like Braden said, they were both adults. Braden knew Wes couldn't deal with a relationship, and he doubted Braden would want one anyway. Why would he? He'd known from the first night he went home with Braden that what they did was a regular occurrence for him.

He turned to the sink to rinse his plate.

"You're thinking too damn hard over here. Stop it before I spank you," Braden whispered in his ear before moving away.

Wes's skin warmed, remembering just how good the man was with his mouth. "Good luck trying that."

Jessie asked if Braden could stay awhile, so he did. They

played a couple games of Go Fish before Wes got Jessie ready for bed. She went easily, like she always did, and when he came out, Braden was finishing up the dishes.

Jesus, who the hell was this guy? He'd never known anyone like him before. "You didn't have to do that."

Braden shrugged. "Wasn't a big deal. Wanna sit outside a bit before I go?"

It didn't come as a surprise to Wes that he did.

"You're frowning," Braden said.

"No I'm not."

"Yes you are."

"Do you enjoy arguing with people?" Wes asked. When he realized he now smiled, he tried to cover it.

Braden just nodded toward the door. "Have a drink with me, Wes."

So he did. They were quiet as they each nursed a beer on the covered front porch.

Finally, when Wes's was almost finished, he spoke. "Thanks for staying to play with her. I'm sure you had something else you could have been doing tonight." Or someone.

"Nah. I think you're rubbing off on me. I'm becoming a homebody. It's pretty scary. I think Jock is getting depressed about it."

Wes wondered how long it had been since Braden had gone out but didn't ask. He had no business wanting to know.

"Is your real name Wesley?" Braden asked out of the blue.

"Yeah."

"I like it. Can I call you Wesley?" he winked.

"Not if you expect me to answer." And then, because he realized what Braden was doing, he said, "What do you want to talk to me about? You're trying to tease me into a good mood. I..." His stomach dropped out when he realized what it must be. "She's not your responsibility. If you can't watch her anymore, we'll figure something out."

"What? Are you kidding? She keeps me in line. My mouth is a million times better since she started busting my balls. I want to talk to you about Christmas. I know you've been worried, and I know Thanksgiving didn't go well. I thought maybe...fuck, this sounds like more than I mean it to, but it's nothing, okay? I just wanted to tell you, you guys are welcome to go home with me. I spend a few days with my family every year. We have a small football team, so there will be plenty of kids for Jess to play with. I thought…hell, I don't know. I thought maybe a change of scenery might help."

Wes concentrated on the feel of the cold bottle of beer in his hand. He let Braden's words work through his head, making its way through *you're fucking crazy* to *maybe it would be good for Jess…*

"I think Jessie would have fun. They have a lot of property, and my mom is like Santa on crack. It might be a good distraction. That's all this is," Braden said.

Wes turned his way, saw the sincerity there, and it made some of the doubt start to drift away. "I'm not sure. Don't know if that's a good idea for her." And he didn't. Maybe taking her away from Lydia and the kids would make things worse.

"Okay." Braden stood, hesitancy on his face. "Just wanted to put that out there. I better get going." Jock scrambled to his feet, too.

Braden got all the way to the porch door before Wes said, "Thanks. I appreciate that, man."

Braden stopped, turned, and smiled. "You can make it up to me sometime." He winked, and then he was gone.

Chapter Twelve

A few days later, Braden sat in his living room with Jock, flipping through the TV channels. There were plenty of sports on, so he went back and forth between games, trying to get into any of them.

He got up, grabbed some chips, ate a handful, but then put the bag up. Afterward, he put his jacket on to take Jock out, but the damn dog just went pee and then ran back for the house. It wasn't *that* cold out.

Braden tossed a load of laundry in the washing machine and decided right then and there that he needed to get out of the house. If he washed clothes when he still had a week's worth left, he definitely had a problem.

He went to his room and flopped onto his bed before dialing up Wes. If Braden needed to get out, Wes definitely did. He doubted that man had done much of anything since the night they'd met and gone home together months ago.

Wes answered with a, "Hello."

"I was sitting here thinking."

"Dangerous of you."

He almost mentioned the fact that Wes joked around with him without being prompted but didn't want to ruin it. "Ha ha, smart guy." Braden chuckled. "But I was thinking you've never experienced the good time that is going out with Braden Roth. I mean, the night we met there was too much drama between you, Noah and Cooper for you to get the full experience. I'm a good time. Ask anyone and they'll tell you." He petted Jock's head when the dog laid it on his stomach.

"Oh wow. A night out with Braden Roth? I've heard they're considering making those a national event. It's heartbreaking that I have to miss it," Wes teased.

Why didn't that answer surprise him? He scratched behind Jock's ear, feeling bummed all of a sudden. "Go out with me, Wes. We'll call Noah and Coop and have them go, too. I'll kick your ass in a few games of pool. We can check out the bar that used to be

Rowdies. I can't remember what it's called now. The new owner just opened her back up. It's opening weekend, actually. I heard they have dollar beers."

"Braden—"

"I'm driving Jock crazy. He's practically shoving my ass out the door. I'm bored. I haven't gone out in too long."

There was a pause, and then Wes said, "No one's keeping you from going out. I told you if watching Jessie interferes then you didn't have to do it."

Braden groaned. "That's not what I mean and you know it. There's nothing wrong with having a little fun once in a while. It's okay to go out. You know Lydia wouldn't mind watching her."

"Not your call, man. Lydia already helps me watch her during the week. She has her own kids. It's not right to push Jessie off on her on the weekends, too."

He closed his eyes, trying not to get too annoyed. He just wanted Wes to have a good time. What was so wrong with that? "That's not what it is and you know it. I'm not asking you on a date. Don't worry, I'm not going to try and get past your defenses, Wes. Christ, I want to go have a fucking beer and hang out with a friend. Stop using Jessie as an excuse."

"Fuck you, Braden. Did you ever think maybe today was a bad day for her? Not everything is about you."

The line went dead. Braden struggled not to throw his phone across the room. He hadn't even thought of that.

Open mouth, insert foot.

***

"What do you guys think of the place?" The bartender crossed his arms, his eyes going from Coop, to Noah, then Braden. He waited for Braden to reply.

Braden looked around the building. They'd obviously done a lot of remodeling. Everything was brand new, modern, and the place was packed as hell. A band played up front, the dance floor busy. They'd doubled the amount of pool tables, and he didn't get a splinter when he sat down like he used to. That was a plus. "Looks good. The place needed a revamp." Braden took a drink of his beer and the bartender grabbed him another one.

"I'm Mason."

"Braden." He pointed next to him. "This is Noah, and that guy at the end is Cooper. He likes running into burning buildings without any gear or backup. That explains the sling."

Noah laughed loudly and Coop shook his head. "Fucker. Don't tell me you wouldn't have done the same thing."

Coop had him there. "Except the getting hurt part. I would have avoided that."

Both Mason and Noah laughed this time.

"I'm glad you like it," Mason told Braden. "Let me know if you have any suggestions. Figured the locals would know more about what you guys are looking for than me."

He'd heard about Mason moving to town a few months ago, when he bought the bar. He hadn't seen him before tonight, though. "Sure thing."

Mason stalled a minute before walking away. Both Noah and Cooper started laughing again as soon as he did.

"What?" Braden asked.

"Tell me you're kidding," Coop said. It was obvious he didn't plan to elaborate, so Braden turned to Noah.

"Your boyfriend is pissing me off."

"Mason has had his eyes on you all night. He's definitely interested. You didn't notice?"

No. "Yeah. Just not in the mood." He leaned back in the chair. "I was an asshole to Wes. I didn't mean to be, but fuck, I just wanted the guy to have a good time. You can't blame me for that." But as usual, he didn't think before he spoke. Didn't think about the fact that because Braden had always just got up and gone when he wanted, others didn't have it so easy.

"All he does is work and take care of Jess. I mean, I respect him for it. Jesus, he's a good guy. I don't know if I could handle that shit. But hell, he needs to get out of the house a little, too. What the fuck are you guys looking at?" Both Noah and Cooper had their eyes trained on him.

Neither of them spoke for a minute before Cooper pushed to his feet. "Come on, buddy, go play a game of pool with me."

"You're wearing a sling." He drank more of his beer.

"I started rehab and I'm allowed to take it off and work it a little. I'll be fine."

"It's your arm." Braden shrugged and stood. He could use a game or two. "You coming?" he asked Noah.

"No, I'm going to take care of something. I'll catch you guys soon." He gave Cooper a quick kiss before walking out.

"Come on. Let's go play," he told Coop, grateful for the

distraction.

***

Wes hadn't been lying when he told Braden that Jessie had a bad day. Most of the time she was fine, but she had days where she just missed her mom, where her young brain tried to make sense of why her heart hurt so much.

Today had been one of them.

But for the past couple hours, even before Braden called, she started to be her typical, happy self again. They made hot chocolate and he let her put as many marshmallows in it as she wanted, and they talked about maybe getting a puppy. She loved Jock, and Wes figured it would be good for her to have a dog to call her own.

So, though he'd been telling the truth, his words to Braden had been partially an excuse as well. Braden was right. He hadn't done anything since before they lost Chelle.

There's nothing wrong with having a little fun once in a while.

"Hey, Jess?" Wes kneeled in front of her as she sat at the table, coloring. "How would you feel about hanging out with your cousins and aunt Lydia tonight? It's okay if you don't want to, but—"

She dropped her crayon. "Sure! I like the bunk bed. We turn it into a fort. Can I get a bunk bed?"

Well that had been easy. "I don't know about the bunk bed, but I'm sure Lydia will let you make the fort with theirs."

She jumped up before he could say anything else and started shoving her feet into shoes and looking for her jacket. Apparently aunt Lydia's house was much more fun than theirs. Was he really that boring? Sure he didn't go out a lot or always have something funny to say, but he wasn't that bad to be around. "I'm going to go pack your clothes, kiddo."

While he got everything in a backpack for her, he called Lydia, who he knew wouldn't mind watching her. She of course said yes, so after Jessie was all packed, Wes jumped into his car and drove her over.

He hardly got a hug out of her before she ran into the room for one of her cousins to make a fort for her.

"So what are you doing tonight?" Lydia rose a brow at him. Her husband clapped Wes on the shoulder and laughed, as if to say, *good luck, man.*

Wes shrugged. "Just felt like getting out of the house. I'm going to go play some pool or something."

Lydia mixed some pudding in a bowl. "She likes Braden a lot."

The hairs on the back of his neck stood. Why did his sister always feel the need to stick her nose in his life? "She does."

"Do you?"

"Lyd… Don't. Plus, how irresponsible of me would it be to get into a relationship with a man so soon after losing Chelle? When things fall to shit, she's the one who would suffer."

She turned to face him. "*When*? You can't even say *if.* Why does it automatically have to be *when*?"

That was his cue that he needed to leave. Wes walked over and kissed his sister on the forehead. "Thank you for everything. I'm going to go."

She sighed. "People love you, Wes. Don't try and make it so hard. Stop pushing people away."

He knew with that she didn't mean Braden. "You're my sister. You know I love you."

"Knowing and feeling it are two different things, though."

"Do you even care, Wes? Honestly, do you give a shit that I'm leaving? I can't be in a relationship where the other person won't

let me in. Not anymore."

He ignored those memories of Alexander. "Thanks for keeping Jess tonight. I'll call you tomorrow."

She shook her head and he gave her a hug before walking out. He ran home real quick to change before heading out again. When he put his hand on the doorknob to open the door, someone knocked.

Wes found himself smiling. Fucking Braden. The man never gave up. He pulled the door open.

"You look a little disappointed to see me," Noah told him.

"Just surprised."

"I came to drag your ass out of the house. Maybe you didn't realize it, but they have dollar beers."

Wes laughed, and it felt good. Braden was right. He needed a night with his friends. "Where do you think I'm going?"

Wes grabbed his jacket and stepped outside.

"Ride with me." Noah headed toward Coop's truck and Wes followed.

He knew Braden must have said something to him. If not,

Noah wouldn't have been here. If he'd been sitting with his sister, she would have been throwing questions at him too fast for him to answer. Thankfully, he didn't have to worry about that with Noah.

It didn't take them long to get to the bar. The parking lot was packed, music thumping through the building.

"Looks like opening weekend is going well," Wes told him.

"Yeah, it looks great inside. The owner's some guy named Mason. He was flirting with Braden and the man didn't even realize it."

Wes got a foreign, tight feeling in his gut. "Yeah."

Noah chuckled. The bastard. He knew exactly what he was doing. He might not come out and ask questions like Lydia would, but he definitely played the game. "Good to know. Maybe I can plan a threesome with them tonight."

Noah let out a loud laugh. "Point taken. I'm minding my own business. Be glad I don't try and get under his skin like you did the first night you met Coop."

He'd been pretty drunk that night. Wes had a beer or two sometimes, but he wasn't much of a drinker, so it didn't take him much to get drunk. "Blame the alcohol. And I've fucked Braden twice. That's all there is. It's not the same thing as you and

Cooper."

"Twice?" Noah cocked a brow.

"Have you always been so nosey?"

"Again, point taken." Noah parked the truck and they got out. They made it to the door before he said, "But I'm here. If you ever need to talk, I'm here."

Wes nodded. He knew that, and appreciated it.

Chapter Thirteen

"Do you play any better when you haven't had an arm injury?" Braden poked Coop in the side with his pool stick.

"Funny. You're a regular comedian. Oh look. Noah got your boyfriend to come out tonight."

Braden turned to look behind him as Wes and Noah headed their way, each with a beer in hand. There had been laughter in Cooper's voice. He'd said something that Braden himself would have said but it still rubbed him the wrong way. He crossed his arms, taking Wes in. Those muscular legs wrapped up in denim that, if he had it his way, he'd remove.

He wore a long-sleeved shirt with the sleeves pushed up his arms. Damn it, he'd always had a thing for forearms. Loved the muscles there, the masculinity of them, the brushing of dark hair.

The asshole of course had to look good tonight.

"So it just takes Noah to get you out of the house, huh? I'll have to remember that." Braden leaned against the pool table. Wes stopped right in front of him.

"Jealous?"

"Maybe a little." He made an inch with his finger and thumb.

Wes's brows drew together as though he didn't expect that reply. "I was on my way here when he showed."

Braden grinned and held out the cue for him. "I knew there had to be a reasonable explanation. I'm Braden Roth, remember?" Wes took the stick from him and Braden continued, "Wanna play?

Wes moved closer to the table. "Yeah, yeah I do."

They played a few games of pool, sometimes Wes and Braden against Noah and Coop, and one game with just Wes and himself. Braden stopped drinking as soon as Wes arrived, because two things became very clear.

First, Wes was in the mood to drink.

Second, the man couldn't handle his alcohol for shit.

He wasn't a sloppy, crazy drunk, but…hell, it was almost like it just unlocked him a little. As though he didn't keep himself so closed off when he had a little drink in him. He kept close to Braden and laughed a lot, and made the rest of them laugh, too.

They moved to a small table where the four of them sat down and bullshitted. Mason made his way to the table at some point, bringing them another pitcher of beer.

"Where are you from?" Wes leaned back in his chair and asked.

"Denver. I owned a few restaurants out there but got sick of the city. Sold 'em all and moved here." He wiped his hands on a towel before slinging it over his shoulder. "What about you guys?"

They went down the line, Cooper explaining he'd lived here since he was a kid, Braden that he'd been here almost a year, followed by Noah then Wes. There was only one other person working the bar, so Mason excused himself after that.

Wes leaned toward him. "Noah was right. He wants you."

"Most people do." Braden winked at him.

Wes punched him in the leg but Braden grabbed onto his wrist, holding Wes's hand there, and damned if he didn't just let it rest on Braden's inner thigh.

Noah and Cooper mumbled something about going somewhere or doing something, but Braden wasn't really paying attention. He just knew they'd left them alone.

"How's the Squirt?" Braden asked.

"Turning her cousin's room into a fort. She was pretty damn happy to get out of the house." His voice was slightly somber when he spoke.

"Eh. Don't take it personal. Forts are pretty cool."

He smiled when Wes laughed.

Under the table, Braden locked his fingers through Wes's as they rested on his leg. He turned when he heard a familiar laugher and saw that a few of the guys from the firehouse came in and were seated at the bar.

"Am I allowed to be glad you came?" he said to Wes.

"When I'm drunk, you're pretty much allowed to do whatever you want."

He had this sexy, sweet, loopy look in his eyes. His brown hair messier than it usually was. The urge to rub his cheek against Wes's facial hair hit him. Jesus, he liked seeing Wes like this. Hated the fact that he had to be drunk to feel free, but Braden couldn't stop staring at him, either. He was all responsibility, seriousness, but right now he was just...Wes. He realized that he liked Wes a little more than he'd thought.

"Dance with me, Wesley." Braden nodded toward the dance floor as a slow song played.

Wes frowned. "There's guys from your firehouse here. Cooper said he didn't know you were bi until he got with Noah, and that no one at the station knows. I just assumed it was something you wanted to keep to yourself."

Braden didn't work that way. He was right that none of them knew, but it wasn't because he purposefully kept it to himself; he just hasn't been with any men in Blackcreek until Wes. "Nah. I'd have to give a shit what other people think for me to want to keep it to myself—which I don't, if you were wondering. You're sexy as hell and I want to dance with you. You're much more agreeable when you're drunk, so this might be my only chance."

He waited for Wes to say no. Waited for life and responsibilities and whatever it was that Wes kept hidden behind his walls to reemerge. But it didn't. Without letting go of his hand, Wes stood and led Braden to the dance floor.

***

When was the last time he danced? Wes couldn't even

remember. He and Alexander had gone out once in a while at the very beginning of their relationship, but it hadn't been long after they'd gotten together that Chelle got sick the first time. It hadn't been as bad then, and she'd fought hard and beat it. But he'd also flown back to Colorado on a lot of his long weekends off to see her. That had put a damper on them going out too much, and once Chelle got healthy again, it just never picked up.

Wes used to love to dance. Loved the feel of another man's body against his, his hands on muscled back, chests touching, music playing, others packed around him doing the same thing.

It was erotic as hell, and he hadn't even realized he missed it until Braden asked him to dance.

They found an empty spot. He wrapped his arms around Braden, who did the same to him, and just let himself feel. Feel the heat of another man, the strength and muscles and masculinity. Took in the woodsy scent and the feel of facial hair against his skin.

Braden's hands traced paths up and down his back as they moved together. In this moment, he didn't have any of the other shit on his mind. Chelle was still here and Jessie was happier and he didn't wish like hell it wasn't so hard to let people in.

"I love to dance," he found himself saying.

"Yeah? Then I'm glad I asked. It's not as hard to make you happy as you want to believe."

Did he want to be hard to please? No, he didn't. But he knew Braden was right about one thing, he didn't always let himself take pleasure in all the things he should.

"You know I've only danced with one other man besides you?"

That statement almost made Wes stumble. He forgot sometimes that Braden was bisexual. Logically he realized he'd just brought it up before they danced, but when he thought about how Braden touched him right now, and the two times they'd been together, it just didn't always compute.

"Do you have a preference?" he found himself asking, knowing that he wouldn't if he wasn't tipsy.

"No."

"Bullshit. When you see your future, do you picture a man or a woman?"

"You volunteering?" Braden asked. When Wes froze up, he added, "Relax. I'm kidding."

Not ready to let go, aware that the song had changed and gone into another slow one, he made himself chill out and waited for Braden to continue.

"Like I said before, it's not really like that. You know me, man. It's not as though I've put a lot of thought into settling down and starting a family someday. I'm not adverse to it if it happens, but I'm not out there looking for it, either. But I guess if I'm thinking about my future, it matters less if it's a man or a woman and more how they make me feel and how I feel about them. Sexually, I love being with men and I enjoy being with women, too. There are differences—things about a man I fucking love and I enjoy the softness of a woman sometimes, too. But if we're talking, what, love? Then I guess that's what matters—who I fall in love with. The rest is just details."

He envied the way Braden saw the world, the fact that he didn't play by any set of rules other than his own.

"Life is short." He brushed a finger over the back of Wes's neck. "I want to be around people who make me happy, and who I do the same thing to. Someone who can handle me," he laughed. "You and I both know that person might not be out there, and I'm okay with that, too. There's a whole lotta fun to be had in this world, Wesley."

Braden pulled back. On reflex, Wes fisted his hand in Braden's shirt, not wanting him to break the connection. Braden didn't let go of him, though, just looked him in the eyes and said, "You wanna have some fun with me tonight? I'm definitely in the mood to have fun with you."

Like he seemed to do so much around Braden, he laughed. "I'm not sure if you're up for the challenge. Once I start to sober up after drinking, all I want to do is go to sleep." He got drunk quick and sobered quick. He'd always been that way.

"I promise you, I'm up for it. Come on. Let's go home so I can show you just how up to it I am." He put his mouth to Wes's ear. "The faster we get out of here, the faster I can fuck you."

Wes's blood ran hot, and shot straight to his dick. That sounded like the kind of fun he *needed* to have.

Chapter Fourteen

Wes had his hands all over Braden as he drove to Wes's house. "I could get used to this side of you," he said into the darkened truck.

"Always talking." Wes's hand slid up Braden's inner thigh and cupped the bulge between his legs.

"Fuck!" The truck jerked slightly. "It's snowing. You're going to make me wreck the truck, and I'll have to explain to the officers that my hard-on felt more important than keeping my ass on the road."

At that, Wes jerked back. Somehow, Braden knew exactly why. "Hey." He reached over to pat Wes's chest with the back of his hand. "I'm kidding. I'm not going to wreck. We're good."

Wes played it off like that wasn't what he'd been upset about, but he also kept his distance from Braden the rest of the ride, too. Braden and his fucking mouth.

The second they got inside, Wes kissed him, though. *Fuck yes.* Braden pushed his tongue past Wes's lips as they stumbled backward, toward the room. He pulled at Wes's jacket, ripping it off and tossing it to the floor.

His mouth went right back on Wes's the second it was gone, but then he realized he needed to get the shirt out of the way, too. "Fuck. You make me lose my head." He chuckled as he shoved his hands under Wes's shirt and pushed it up his body. Braden finally got rid of it, his heart beating crazy with lust as he tried to kiss Wes again. Only this time, Wes did stumble, falling back onto the bed. Braden went down with him, both of them laughing.

"You're not allowed to move anymore, ya drunk bastard. Lay there and let me do what I want to you."

Braden let his tongue circle around Wes's bellybutton before he licked his way up the man's chest and his hand slid down to cover the bulge behind his fly.

Wes hissed. "Fuck."

Yeah, he liked hearing that word out of Wes's mouth, and knowing he was responsible for it.

"Fuck!" Wes said again.

Braden stilled, suddenly not liking the sound of the word. "What?"

"My cell is in your truck. I need to get it in case Jess wakes up in the middle of the night or something."

Those words made Braden pause. He wasn't sure why they hit him right in the chest, but they did. They hit him so hard it felt like they knocked the wind out of him. How easy would it be to leave the phone out there? She was with her aunt. Or they could fuck and then get it, but Wes wouldn't do that. Wouldn't do it because of how much he loved the little girl and wanted to do right by her. Had he ever been that selfless?

Wes tried to stand, but Braden put a hand on his chest and held him down. Wes looked up at him with those whiskey-colored eyes of his, and they made that punch to his chest happen again. Not the kind that hurt; just letting him know someone was there.

"I'll go." He leaned forward and kissed him. "You're already half naked, you might as well finish. Take your clothes off and wait for me. I really want your cock in my mouth again before I fuck you."

Wes groaned as though it was painful for Braden to leave him. He had to admit he liked the sound. It seemed as though he liked a lot of what came out of Wes's mouth, *and* how he used it.

Braden scrambled to his feet and went out the door. He made it all the way to his truck before he realized he didn't have his keys. "Fuck!" He ran back to the house, and found them on the floor by the door where he must have dropped them.

His interior light was out, so it took him a few minutes to find the phone where it slid under the seat. His dick ached the whole time. The things he couldn't wait to do to Wes. He told the man he wanted to suck him off, but he wanted his ass, too. Wanted to taste it before he fucked him, because he had yet to do that.

He already started unbuttoning and unzipping his pants as he turned for Wes's small room.

And stopped in the doorway. Wes had made it as far as getting his pants off before he passed out in a pair of black boxer-briefs. The tight ass that Braden had just been thinking about right there. Long muscles flexed in his back as he lay with his head to the side, dead to the world.

Aaaannnd, there went his erection. Not that he didn't still want to fuck Wes senseless, but he couldn't wake him, either. It wasn't right.

Grumbling the whole time, Braden pulled the blanket up and covered Wes, thought about climbing into bed with him but knew he wouldn't do that. It wasn't right to stay when he knew Wes didn't do that.

He made sure the ringer was up on Wes's phone before setting it on the bedside table. "I'm not done with you yet. You owe me," he groaned out. But then he stopped, looked at him. Saw the lines in his forehead relaxed as they only ever really were when he came. Or, Braden guessed, while he slept. Saw him relaxed in a way Wes rarely let himself be.

The man tried to carry the world on his shoulders, and one day it would break him.

"Sleep well." Braden ran a hand through Wes's hair, watched him for another second, looked at the tattoo on Wes's arm that surprised him for some reason. Wes didn't seem like the tattoo type. Finally, he hit the lights on his way out. He made a quick stop in the kitchen first. Afterward, he locked up Wes's house and went home with an aching cock, knowing it wouldn't be the first time he jacked off to the thought of Wes.

***

Wes's eyes burned as he slowly pried them open. The second the sandpaper eased up, the night before came back to him.

He'd gotten drunk.

Danced with Braden.

Had a good time with Braden.

Really wanted to be fucked by Braden.

And then had passed out on Braden. Well, not *on* him, unfortunately, because then maybe that would have meant he'd gotten thoroughly fucked.

Groaning, he rolled over to see his phone on the bedside table. At the same time, he realized he was covered up, the lights were off, and Braden was gone. He could have stayed. Probably should have stayed. But he hadn't. *Because I told him I don't stay the night...*

He groaned again when he realized it was only six a.m. What the hell was he doing up so early?

There were no calls from Lydia. Unable to go back to sleep, Wes pushed out of bed. His first stop was the bathroom to brush his teeth.

He could have woken me up. Why did he let me sleep?

The lights in the rest of the house were out, too, no doubt another Braden move.

He struggled to understand the man sometimes. He was full of contradictions. So carefree and wild in so many ways. He mostly thought about having fun, and other than work, he didn't have any responsibilities. But then in other ways…hell, had he ever really known someone who thought about others as much as Braden did? From showing up at the service, to helping with Jess, and the way he respected Wes and his fucked up ways.

"Six is way too early to be thinking so hard," he mumbled on his way to the kitchen. Wes stopped when he saw the note on the coffee pot.

Just push Start.

Chuckling to himself, he pushed the start button and, sure enough, coffee started brewing. He would have never thought to do something like that for someone. But Braden had.

For him.

Wes opened the cabinet for a coffee cup.

Drink coffee. Relax. Stop overthinking how fucking sweet I am.

Wes hadn't even realized he felt heaviness in his limbs, in his whole damn body, until it started to drift away. But somehow, looking at Braden's notes, it just…went. Did he always feel that weighed down? All he knew was, when he looked at that note, he didn't. He felt good.

And he didn't want that to go away.

Without letting himself think about it, Wes turned off the coffee pot. He took the world's quickest shower, then went straight for his room, got dressed in whatever he could find, grabbed his jacket and went straight for the door.

Luckily, Braden's house wasn't too hard to find. He'd only been here once, and walked back to the bar in the middle of the night.

He felt sort of on edge. No, more like he was high on something. What, he didn't know, but his body was jittery and eager as he pounded on the door.

Wes ignored the internal questions asking him what the hell he was doing here. Ignored the thoughts telling him to turn and go, because all he wanted right now was to laugh, and fuck, and forget everything in his life except for the things that made him feel good. Braden was the only person who could give him that.

Jock started going crazy inside. Patience left him as he banged on the door again, needing…hell, he didn't know what.

It was a minute later that Braden jerked the door open, wearing nothing but a pair of sweats. His golden skin taut across firm muscles. His hair was a mess, his eyes swollen from lack of sleep, but still he cocked a brow when he saw Wes. The right side of his mouth rose, and Wes suddenly wanted to kiss the smirk off his face.

"Miss me?" Braden asked.

"Want you," Wes replied.

That was all it took for Braden to open the door wider and signal for him to go in. Wes closed the door behind them and turned to see Braden heading for the hallway, taking off his sweats as he went. He left them right on the floor, the tattoo on his back and his round, hard ass on perfect display as he went.

"You coming?" he asked after turning around. Wes felt like an amateur, nerves he hadn't felt since he was a teenager rising inside him.

"I hope to be soon," he forced himself to say, getting another of Braden's smiles.

"That's what I like to hear. You're funny when you want to be, Wesley."

"Don't call me that." Still, Wes took a step forward.

"Are you going to make me stop?" Braden asked, and then he

was moving down the hallway. Wes went right behind him, eager electricity bouncing around inside him.

"You're going to have to stay out, buddy," Wes told Jock as he closed the bedroom door. Before he could move, Braden pushed him against the door from behind, Braden's chest against his back.

Learning forward, he put his mouth close to Wes's ear. "I jerked off thinking about you last night."

"Sorry I missed it."

Braden pushed into him, rubbed his cock against Wes's ass. It was a shock to his system, making his senses explode.

"Oh *fuck,*" Wes gritted out when Braden pulled his shirt and jacket away from his neck and bit into it.

"I'm glad you came," he whispered.

Fuck if Wes wasn't glad, too.

Chapter Fifteen

Well, Braden hadn't expected that. He wasn't complaining—definitely not—but he hadn't expected Wes to show up. "Wanted your ass last night." He palmed a cheek. "But you passed out on me, and now you're here because you want me? Mmm, maybe after I have you first."

Wes's fingers fumbled with his button and Braden turned him to help, stopping only when Wes said, "I'm here so you can fuck me."

Damned if those words didn't make a shiver race down Braden's spine, making fire shoot through his veins. "Greedy little bottom." He forced his fingers to work as he unbuttoned Wes's jeans and shoved the zipper down. As he did, Wes took his jacket off then pulled his shirt over his head.

The second he was naked, Braden wrapped a hand around his thick erection, rubbed his thumb over the head, spreading the pre-come there.

Wes hissed.

"I'd suck you off, but I wouldn't want to stop. Lay on the bed."

He followed Wes over. As the other man lay down, Braden grabbed his waist and pulled. "Edge of the bed." He dropped to his knees and pushed Wes's legs toward his stomach.

"Oh, fuck," Wes mumbled, hunger in his voice.

"Don't pretend you don't want it," Braden teased before rubbing Wes's ring with his finger. His cock jerked and he noticed Wes's did the same. "We both know I like fucking. You've discovered how much I love giving head, but I like this, too."

Again, he let his finger explore, no penetration, just rubbing Wes's pucker back and forth.

"Always talking." Wes wrapped a hand around his own erection.

"Wait. Not yet." Braden pushed his hand away. "I want to be the one to pleasure you."

"Then do it."

Braden couldn't help but laugh. "You're pushy when you're horny. I like it."

With that, Braden leaned forward, ran his tongue from Wes's hole to his balls and back down again. "Hold your legs," he told Wes before his tongue went to work on him again.

Wes did as he said, keeping his legs up and out of the way as Braden tongued him. He used his hand to cup Wes's sac as he worked him.

Every one of Wes's moans urged him on, made him want to give him more pleasure than he'd ever had.

Braden sucked his finger before pushing it inside. He watched as his finger slid in and out of Wes's body. "That is so fucking sexy. I can't wait until it's my cock." And then he leaned in again, using his tongue and finger on him at the same time.

"Yeah...Oh fuck," Wes groaned as he latched onto Braden's hair, pushing his head closer to him.

"So fucking pushy," Braden said as he curved his finger, looking for Wes's prostate.

"Don't." Wes grabbed his wrist. "I don't want to come yet.

Fuck me."

Braden pushed to his feet. Pre-come already pearled at the tip of his cock. Jesus, this man did it for him. "You don't have to ask me twice." He grabbed lube and a condom from his bedside table. Once he had himself covered, he squirted some lube in his hand, rubbed some on himself and then on Wes's asshole.

"Don't move," he told Wes. "I want you right there." Then he ran his hand down Wes's chest, let his fingers run through the hair there, just touching. Always touching…

He traced Wes's abs with his finger. "You're too damn sexy."

"You're still talking."

Braden shook his head, leaned over Wes's body and pushed inside. "You like it when I talk."

Before Wes could argue with him, Braden pulled out and shoved forward again. He took Wes's mouth, owning it as he thrust as long and deep as he could.

Wes's feet dug into Braden's legs as he pumped, as Wes's body squeezed his cock oh so fucking right.

It felt like someone injected pleasure into him, needles in every inch of his body, yet he still wanted more.

"Harder." Wes's grip on him tightened. "I want more."

Christ, that almost made him come right there. Braden growled as he jerked out of him, as he flipped Wes over to lie on his stomach before pushing inside again. Leaning over his back, he slammed into him.

This time when Wes's hand moved down, he didn't stop Wes from jerking himself off. He tried to position them so he had more space without stopping his movements, wanting as deep inside him as he could get.

"Fuck, my whole body is aching. I'm about to fucking lose it, Wesley." He thread his arms under Wes's from behind and let his hands grip his shoulders. It gave him the leverage he needed.

Wes's hand moved faster, then he groaned, his body jerking in completion under Braden. It was all he needed to knock him over the edge, too. His cock jerked inside Wes as he continued to pump through his orgasm. When his body felt bled dry, he rolled off Wes and onto the bed. His chest heaved in and out. He remembered Wes's words when he'd arrived, how he wanted to come soon. Braden let his head roll to the side, to see whisky eyes looking at him. "Was that soon enough?"

***

"Do you ever stop?" Wes almost turned away after asking the

question but for some reason he couldn't, so he just lay there, watching Braden.

"Will you ever stop pretending you want me to?" he countered.

Who the hell was this man? Half the time he didn't know how to respond to him, and Wes wasn't sure how he felt about that. Just like with the notes this morning, or the fact that Braden had left him last night because he'd known Wes would have wanted him to, it made conflicting emotions war inside him—respect, and the urge to flee.

Which was why he tried not to think of it at all. Luckily for him, his stomach growled loudly enough for Braden to hear.

"I made ya work up an appetite, huh?"

"No. I'm always hungry after a night of drinking. Not everything is about you." He surprised himself when he playfully pushed at Braden's arm. "I should go—"

"Stay there. Since it was your need for me that forced you out of bed so early, I at least owe you some food." Braden winked as he stood. He headed toward the bathroom in his room.

Wes rolled to his side and watched as Braden got rid of the condom and then washed his hands. As he moved, the muscles constricted in his body. He was long and thin, but ripped, too. All man. It really should be illegal to be that sexy. So sexy that Wes didn't even have the strength to call him on his cockiness.

"Coffee?" Braden asked.

"I should go," Wes replied, but the words sort of stuck in his mouth like peanut butter. He didn't want to mutter them.

"Eh, it's fun to do something you shouldn't every once in a while. Give me like five and I'll be right back. Don't move. Or get dressed. I like the view." Braden turned and walked out of the room.

And to his shock, Wes didn't get up to leave. His head spun half the time he was with the man. He'd try to compute one thing he said but Braden would already be moving to the next.

Needing to do something, Wes grabbed his pants, pulled his cell out and checked for any calls. It was still early, so he set the phone on Braden's bedside table and…sat there. Just sat in the middle of Braden's bed, waiting for him.

What the fuck am I doing?

"Here." Braden stuck his head around the corner and held out two plates. Wes grabbed them and saw massive cinnamon rolls on each one. It was enough to make his mouth water.

"Cream and sugar?" Braden asked.

"Um, yeah. Thanks, man."

"No problem. I'll be right back." He nodded his head toward the bed again.

"Jesus, you're pushy."

"No, that's you." Braden ducked out of the room again and Wes found himself back on the bed, this time with plate-sized cinnamon rolls.

It wasn't a minute later before Braden came back in with napkins and their coffee, handing one cup to Wes and setting his on the table.

"If you have to be up at this hour, there's no better way to do it than sex, coffee, and sugar." Braden cocked his brow before popping a piece of food into his mouth.

For once, Wes couldn't argue with him.

Together, they sat on the middle of Braden's bed, naked and eating. Neither of them really spoke until Wes set their plates on the table.

"So," Braden leaned back, arms outstretched behind him, hands on the bed. "Where'd you go to school? I know you're from

Colorado, right? But then you left?"

"Yeah. We didn't live in Blackcreek, but I'm from Colorado. I went to California not long after high school. Went to college there, and I stayed there until I moved here. What about you?"

"Grew up outside of Denver. Like I told you, my parents have a shit-ton of land. Lived in a small town, and the second I could get my ass outta there, I did."

Wes leaned back against the headboard with his legs out in front of him. "You didn't like it?"

Braden's forehead wrinkled as though he was confused. "I liked it fine. It was a good place to grow up—just not where I wanted to live forever. I bailed with a buddy of mine right after graduation. Moved around a bit, then ended up in Seattle for a while. It was my favorite there. Have you ever been?"

Wes shook his head. He'd been to California and Colorado. That was it.

"Ah, there are good times to be had there."

"Yeah, I've heard they have some nice art galleries out there. I'd love to visit some." It wasn't something he'd ever really thought he'd do. Now, well he doubted he'd be going much of anywhere. Not that being here with Jessie wasn't more important, because it was, but still…why hadn't he ever tried to go anywhere before?

"I forgot you paint. When are you going to paint me something, Picasso?"

Wes chuckled and shook his head. "I don't paint anymore."

"You could paint."

"But I don't."

"But you could."

Damn, the man acted like he was ten sometimes. "Why do you always try to argue with me? You're always bustin' my balls for something, or trying to get under my skin. Like that 'Wesley' bullshit. I asked you not to call me that."

Braden moved closer to him. "Because it's fun to watch you get all rattled, to pretend shit bugs you more than it does. I'm not sure you even know you're pretending, though."

Was he right? No. Wes didn't pretend stuff bothered him. Why would anyone do that? He didn't want to feel like shit most of the time, he just did.

Braden settled himself between Wes's legs. He leaned on one of his arms, which was on the outside of Wes, wrapped around behind him. Their faces were close, Braden's legs over Wes's left one and the other knee angled up.

Wes could never imagine doing that, just putting himself in someone's space like that, but Braden did it, and Wes didn't push him away.

Braden grinned up at him, his fingers tickling the back of Wes's waist. "You like me."

Wes rolled his eyes. "I like fucking you."

"Nope. You like me. You like that I get under your skin and never stop talking. I think you might even like it when I call you Wesley."

Wes tried, though not very hard, to get up, but Braden didn't let him. "I don't like it when you call me Wesley." He'd never really liked the name.

"But you like me?" he asked.

Wes let the smile slide off his face. He looked down at Braden, who held his eyes intensely. "Braden—"

Braden leaned forward and pressed his lips to Wes's. And Wes let him. Let him kiss the hell out of him before he pulled back, but didn't move from his spot, wrapped up in Wes.

He was letting Wes off the hook. He knew that. And Wes allowed it. "What did you used to paint?"

"Whatever came into my head."

From there they went to sports. Wes talked about playing baseball in high school and Braden talked about soccer, which he actually still played, and his time playing football, too. They spoke about their jobs next, then more of Braden's adventures, Noah and Cooper, and on and on. The whole time, Braden was always touching, fingers brushing over Wes's back, his leg, his stomach. His leather bracelet rubbing against Wes's skin, too. It was around eleven thirty that his phone rang, Lydia telling him Jessie was ready to go home.

After they got dressed, Braden walked him to the door, saying he had to let Jock out again.

He stood in the driveway as Jock ran around and Wes climbed into his car. "See ya Wednesday." Braden grinned at him.

"See ya." Wes closed the door, turned on the car…then rolled the fucking window down. He wasn't sure what he planned to say until the words just came out. "Thanks…for leaving last night. That's probably a shitty thing to thank someone for, but… yeah. There it is." Braden wouldn't have left. He didn't work that way. He'd done it to be fair to Wes.

"And for the coffee this morning."

"No problem."

As Wes drove off, he realized Braden was right. He did like him, he just didn't know what the hell it meant, or if he'd actually do something about it.

Chapter Sixteen

Braden sat in a chair at the firehouse, arms crossed and his feet kicked up on a table. He expected it when three guys walked up to him, had seen it coming all day, but still didn't look up at them when they stopped in front of him.

"What's up, Roth?" Fred asked him. It was the first time Braden had seen him since the night he'd danced with Wes.

Braden leaned back so he could see their faces. "Not much. Was thinking about texting my buddy Wes to see if he wanted me to bring him something for dinner tonight. You know him, right? I was at the bar with him the other night. He's pretty impossible to miss though, right? I mean, at least for me."

Yeah, he'd never been known for being real subtle. He knew

what they wanted to talk to him about. Fred had always been a homophobic asshole. Coop had told him some shit he'd said before as well.

He didn't give a fuck how they felt about his life. Now they knew where he was coming from, too.

"What the fuck, man?" Fred asked. "You're a fag now, too? First Bradshaw and now you?"

Braden ignored his rapid pulse, stood, and bit back the urge for his fist to meet Fred's face. "I'll let you get by with saying that once, and once only. I don't give a shit if I lose my job or not. You say that again and we're going rounds." He shrugged. "Plus, you don't know what you're talking about. I've been fucking guys much longer than Coop has." With that, Fred charged at him. Gus and Rick both grabbed his arms to hold him back, Rick saying, "Christ, Braden. Have some fucking tact, would ya?"

"Tact? You guys just surrounded me like the fucking mob or something, like it's any of your goddamned business who I'm dating."

Dating? But I'm not really dating him, am I? Not if you asked Wes.

With that Fred jerked out of their grip. "Stay the fuck away from me, Roth. You and Bradshaw both. Fucking queers." And then he stormed away.

Gus shrugged, "Sorry, man. You know how he gets sometimes," before following right behind Fred.

"Fuck!" Braden dropped to the chair, running both his hands through his hair. He would never understand people, never get why it mattered who someone was attracted to or loved. He'd seen too many people he knew getting hell about their preferences for Braden to let it go easily.

"You have to see how we were shocked. We were just curious…he's a fucking dude. I've been out with you when you were with women," Rick said.

"No offense, but fuck you and your curiosity. You didn't come at me like someone curious. And why the hell do you have a right to be curious, anyway?"

"Yeah," Rick nodded. "Yeah, you're right. Just got one question for ya, man." He nudged Braden's arm in a way Braden figured meant he was trying to say they were cool.

"What's that?"

"I know you said you were into guys longer than Coop, but I gotta know…do I need to stop drinking the water around here or what?" he smirked.

Braden stood again and shook his head. "If that was the case, you'd be doing yourself a favor to drink the water." He winked at Rick before walking away.

They didn't get any calls the rest of his shift. He went to the gym when he got off and exercised for a while. Of course he'd been giving Fred shit when he said he'd been about to call Wes for dinner. It didn't mean he didn't kind of want to, but knowing the man, he figured he'd be all pissy because of how they spent their last time together.

How he could be in a bad mood after that morning he didn't know, but knowing Wes, he would be. Or would he think he should be? There was always something right below the surface that Braden saw in him, a little light in his eyes that said he wanted more. Not necessarily from Braden but from life. He just didn't get why Wes wouldn't take it.

Or why I care so much…

But that was a lie, and Braden didn't do that shit. He liked Wes, plain and simple. Liked more than just fucking him. He liked being around him. Liked the way he made Braden feel. And the Squirt, too.

Braden went about his business the rest of the week. On Wednesday he picked Jessie up at preschool like he did every week and took her home.

They watched cartoons and traced her ABCs, and Braden went ahead and made dinner. He texted Wes that he did and then put his phone in his jacket pocket so he could claim he didn't hear it when Wes replied.

It was just a few minutes before Wes would be home when he lay on the floor coloring with Jessie and she asked, "Are you Uncle Wes's boyfriend?"

Oh fuck. He had no idea how to answer that. He wasn't, but usually questions like that came with more questions that Braden wasn't so sure he should be answering.

"Um…no? We're friends."

"Do you like him? I like Eric. I might marry him one day."

"Who is this Eric kid? You're too young to talk about boys. I might need to meet this guy," he teased.

"He's in *The Little Mermaid*, silly!"

"Silly? Silly? I'll show you silly." He reached over and pulled her to him and tickled her. Jessie started screaming and laughing, making Braden laugh, too.

"Are you torturing my niece?" Wes's voice came from the

doorway.

"What?" Braden asked. "She's torturing me!"

"Save me, Uncle Wes!" Jessie scrambled out of his arms and ran for Wes.

"You little sneak! You started this." Braden laughed but watched as Wes bent and Jessie hugged him. His eyes caught Wes's over the little girl's shoulder and he got a reserved smile.

Braden winked at him, a strange need filling him up. A need to be able to embrace the man as a welcome home, the same way Jessie did. A strange need to feel like he belonged with these two people who he enjoyed being around so much.

***

On Saturday morning, Wes stood in the doorway to Chelle's bedroom. Lydia had Jessie because he planned to start going through Chelle's things. He needed to, it was important, but that didn't mean his gut didn't ache at the thought of it.

Lydia offered to do it. Maybe he should have let her, but he felt like this was something he needed to do.

His sister, Jessie's mom, was gone, regardless if he kept her room in tact or not.

He took a step into the room, and then another. Wes eyed the chest but new he couldn't deal with that yet. The thing meant too much to her.

He looked over the pictures on her dresser. It was full of them, mostly of Jessie, but some of the rest of them, too. On the corner, it was the two of them on his high school graduation day.

Wes picked it up. Jesus, he looked so carefree. He'd always been the type to worry—to stress out over things more than most— but that day, nothing could touch him.

Yet, it didn't compare to the smile on Chelle's face. She looked prouder than any mom ever could. She'd always been like that with both him and Lydia, but especially Wes. Their happiness had always meant more to her than her own.

She would hate the way he was living his life. She had hated it before she died. All she'd wanted was for them to all be happy. He'd let her down in life, and now he was doing it in death, too.

He didn't want to let her down, didn't want to let Jessie down, either.

Wes set the picture down, left the room and closed the door behind him. After shoving his feet into shoes and pulling on a jacket, he went for the door, drove straight to Lydia's.

Lydia's eyes stretched wide when he stormed into the house.

"Wes? What's wrong?"

He shook his head. "Nothing, nothing at all," he said before calling out, "Jessie, come here."

Her curls flopped as she ran out of a bedroom and to him. "What's wrong?"

A sharp pain pierced his chest at the question. Almost five was too young to automatically assume the worst.

He kneeled down. "Nothing's wrong. I just want to spend some time with you. I was thinking we could go do something fun. Whatever you want."

Her little face lit up. "Can we go bowling?"

Bowling? He told her they could do whatever she wanted and that's what she chose? "Have you ever been before?"

"No, but Braden says it's fun. He said we should go sometime."

Braden. Damn, he was a good man. He was good with Jessie, and hell…good with Wes, too.

"Yeah, sure. We can go bowling. Now where's your coat?"

He pushed to his feet as Jessie ran toward the hall closet before stopping halfway.

"Can Braden come, too?" she asked.

Wes didn't let himself think before he replied, "We'll call him. If he's free, we'll ask him to come."

The way she smiled, you'd think he just gave her the world. Braden seemed to have that effect on people.

Chapter Seventeen

Braden watched as Wes set Jessie up with the ramp in front of their lane. He tried to set her ball on it for her, but she shook her head and wouldn't let him. Sure enough, Wes handed her the bowling ball and she hefted the thing on the ramp before pushing it.

It felt like it took the damn thing about ten minutes to hit the pins, but Wes and Jessie stood there watching it go the whole time.

Only three pins fell, but that didn't stop Jessie from jumping into Wes's arms before turning and running for Braden. "I did it, Braden. Didja see?"

He hugged her back as she wrapped her little arms around his thigh. "I sure did. You have another turn. Let's see how many you can knock down this time."

With that she was gone, running back to Wes to take her second turn.

It was strange being here with them. Not in the way he would have thought, not that he didn't belong even though this was far from anything he'd done. Yeah, he'd taken his nieces and nephews places before, but he was doing this with the man he'd been sleeping with. The man he wanted to sleep with again.

Needless to say, it put a totally different spin on things.

He sure as shit couldn't believe Wes had invited him.

When Jessie's turn was over, she raced to him and sat down. They both watched as Wes bowled a strike, the fucker.

"Don't tell me you're going to try and beat me, man. I hate to tell you, but it won't happen." Braden clipped Wes with his arm as they passed each other.

"I'm not trying," he replied. "I can promise you I will, though."

Braden laughed. "Oh, you think so? Keep dreaming."

Braden hit a strike, too.

They went back and forth like that the whole game. Jessie clapped and cheered for both of them. She wouldn't let either of them go up with her when she bowled, wanting to do it on her own. Wes got lucky and won the first game. By the second one they'd cooled off a little, but Jessie still took it more seriously than he thought a kid would.

"She's a determined little thing, isn't she?" Braden sat in the seat next to Wes. Their legs touched the seats were so close, yet he didn't scoot over. Wes cocked a brow at him. *Yep, that's right. If I'm too close, you're going to have to move yourself.*

He didn't.

"She gets it from Chelle. She was always just like that. I don't think there was a damn thing she couldn't do."

The pain in Wes's voice tugged at him, called the protective instinct inside Braden. He nudged the man's side with his elbow. "You're determined, too. Nothing you're doing right now is small stuff." Raising a kid was probably the biggest thing there was.

"Stop trying to get into my pants." Wes nudged him back.

"Ah, come on. Don't pretend I have to give you compliments to get there."

Jessie ran up to them before Wes could reply. He narrowed his eyes at Braden, his lip twitching as though he wanted to say something but couldn't.

"It's your turn, Uncle Wes!"

"Yeah. It's your turn." Braden crossed his arms and earned another dirty look from Wes.

They went back and forth in between their turns. When they finished their second game Wes got a bunch of quarters before letting Jessie loose in the small arcade.

While Braden ordered them some food, Wes moved a table under the window in the wall so they were right by the door and could see her.

I never would have thought of that. The thought rubbed him wrong, sandpaper against his skin. It was something so simple, yet if he had been here alone with Jess, he never would have done it. Mostly, he was too busy thinking about himself, or what the next thing he could do was. He'd never really been responsible for much of anything other than his job.

"So what brought this on?" Braden asked him as they sat across from each other at the table.

Wes shrugged, didn't bullshit or pretend he didn't know what Braden meant, and said, "I was supposed to go through Chelle's room. I can't keep it the way it is, but I really fucking want to." He laughed humorlessly before continuing, "I don't know, maybe I just used it as an excuse so I wouldn't have to do something important. Bowling is a whole lot easier than packing away my sister's things, but I thought about Chelle. She'd be doing more with Jessie, and I wanted to do that, too. So I did."

Braden used his foot to touch Wes's leg. "You didn't use it as an excuse. Being with her is more important than anything else."

Wes turned and looked through the glass, watching her. "Yeah, I guess you're right."

"Usually am." He hoped for Wes's half-grin and got it.

"Asshole."

They were quiet for a minute before Braden said, "Thanks."

"For what?" Wes picked up a straw wrapper and rolled it into a ball.

"For telling me that. For inviting me."

Their eyes held each other's and he tried to read what Wes was thinking, wondered what Wes saw in Braden's stare.

"She wanted you to come. She likes you." He flicked the rolled up wrapper at Braden. "And I kind of like you, too. I don't know what that means. I still have a lot going on with Jess, and I haven't let myself…fuck, I haven't really let myself give a shit in a long time, but yeah. There you have it."

That took a lot for Wes to say. The fact that he did, that he wanted Braden to know that, made Braden's heart slam around in his chest. There were so many things he did for fun, but he felt like more than just a good time with them. He felt important. It was as if someone lodged something in Braden's throat. He wanted to speak but couldn't. His chest squeezed and he took a deep breath, forcing himself to speak. "Knew I'd wear you down eventually. I'm Braden Roth, after all."

They both laughed before Wes nodded toward the room. "Let's go play with Jess."

Braden stood and went with him.

***

The ER got too many MVA's to count. Every time his pager went off, Wes knew it was another call, for another car accident. The weather was shit, and people obviously didn't drive very well in it. That didn't count the typical ER patients. He'd listened to so many lungs, given so many breathing treatments, that he thought if he heard the word "lung" one more time today, he'd lose it.

And he still had a decent drive home ahead of himself.

Wes held his hands in front of the heater while his car warmed up. He'd gotten up early this morning to put chains on because he'd known he would need them, so luckily he didn't have to do that.

He wasn't in the car ten minutes before traffic was dead-stopped. Unless he wanted to turn around and take the really long way, this was the only road from the hospital to Blackcreek. He had no doubt there was a wreck somewhere ahead that would delay him who knew how long.

He grabbed his phone from the passenger seat and called Braden.

"Accident?" Was the first word out of Braden's mouth.

"Yep."

"Not yours?"

"Nope."

He heard Braden move around on the other end of the line before he spoke. "We're good here. I don't have anything going on tonight. Take your time and be careful. You wanna talk to her real quick?"

He let out a relieved breath. He didn't know why. He knew

Braden well enough to know that even if he'd had plans, he wouldn't hesitate to cancel them to stay with Jessie.

As if he could read Wes's mind, he said, "Did you think I would be upset? Come on, man. You know me better than that."

Traffic moved about ten feet.

"No. I didn't think that."

"So you're glad I didn't have plans?"

Was he? Is that what it was? He didn't know. "Shut up and let me talk to my niece."

Braden laughed but then added, "When we know the weather is going to be bad, maybe we should switch vehicles. I don't go anywhere other than around town."

Wes's thumb automatically started drumming on the steering wheel. Nausea rolled through him, though he didn't really get the origin of it. "We're not switching vehicles. It's…"

"Something a friend would do for another? It's not really a big deal."

Yes, it was. Normal friends didn't do that. "I've been thinking about trading my car in anyway. I need something to handle the roads better around here." He'd been thinking about it for about five minutes.

"Well that's smart of you. Here, let me grab Jess. She's in her room."

He heard Braden tell her that he was on the phone before Jessie said, "Where are you?"

When traffic moved, he went a little further. "I'm stuck in traffic. They want everyone to go real slow and be extra careful because we got a lot of snow. I'll be home as soon as I can though, okay? Braden might have to put you to sleep tonight. If he does, do you want me to wake you up when I get there?"

Her voice got quiet. "How long will you be?"

"I don't know, kiddo. It's okay, though. I'm fine, and you have fun with Braden. It'll be okay."

"I miss you."

His heart squeezed. "I'll miss you, too. I'll wake you up when I get in. Can you do me a favor?"

"Mm hm."

"Maybe you can help Braden keep an extra close eye on Jock. He's feeling a little sleepy tonight, and we both think you take such good care of Jock. Can you play with him and stuff to help

Braden out?"

She had excitement back in her voice when she said, "Yes!"

"Good girl. I love you."

There was a rustling sound on the phone and then she hung up. She loved that damn dog. He really should get her one. It would be a good distraction for her if she thought she had to take care of Jock for Braden.

The drive home that took half an hour during good weather, forty-five to an hour in decent weather, took him three hours, which meant his usual thirteen-hour day was sixteen. He was dead on his feet when he walked through the door.

Wes hung his jacket on the rack by the door and shook his head when he saw Braden's feet sticking over the arm of the couch with Jock's head resting on them. He moved closer until he could see over the back of the couch. His feet planted on the ground when he could.

Jock and Braden weren't alone on the couch. Jessie was curled up next to him, her head on his chest. A small blanket lay over the top of her, her soft breathing mixing with Braden's.

They both had their eyes closed, dead to the world, the TV muted in the background.

Wes couldn't move. He couldn't stop looking at how relaxed she was with him. How good Braden was with her—this man who admitted many one-night stands; had had one with Wes himself. Who watched cartoons, and stuck his foot in his mouth more often than not, and couldn't sit still half the time. He was here when Wes needed him, and he was here for Jessie. He was pretty sure the man loved his niece.

He closed his eyes, sucked in a deep breath, caught between wanting to grab onto this and run. Alexander had been different than Braden, but they'd had a good relationship. Until he left, the same way almost everyone had left him.

Could he risk that again? Could he risk Jessie's heart?

He didn't know. But still he couldn't stop himself from moving forward. From letting the back of his hand brush over the couple days' growth on Braden's jaw.

His green eyes popped open but Wes didn't move his hand. He touched him again, then his hair. Braden smiled, and it was like a shot to the chest. Not painful, but powerful. The man was so fucking sexy.

"What time is it?" Braden whispered.

"A little after ten."

Braden looked down, then ran a hand over Jessie's curls. "Sorry. She was worried about you."

"No." He shook his head. "Don't be sorry. Let me put her to bed. I'll be right back."

Braden nodded and Wes walked to the other side of the couch and lifted Jessie into his arms. He heard the license on Jock's collar clank and realized the dog followed him.

As soon as he laid Jessie in her bed, her eyes fluttered open.

"I'm home, kiddo. You good?" he asked.

She gave a sleepy nod before closing her eyes again. Jock jumped onto the bed with her and Wes let him stay. He hit the light, kissed her forehead, and then closed the door as he left her room.

Braden had the blanket wrapped around himself, his eyes closed again, when Wes made it to him. Christ, he really fucking wanted to kiss him. Kiss him, fuck him, whatever he could. But instead, he just sat on the table. As soon as he did, Braden opened his eyes. "Didn't mean to pass out again. Let me grab my shit and I'll get going."

Wes closed his eyes, then opened them and shook his head. Braden sat up, right in front of him, their knees pressing against each other's. "You're thinking too hard over there. What's up?" he put a hand on Wes's leg.

Wes didn't pause, just opened his mouth and said one word. "Stay."

Chapter Eighteen

"You don't let people stay." Braden wished like hell he didn't have to say the words. That he could just say "yes" because every fucking nerve ending in his body was screaming for that. It was such a simple thing—to stay the night. He'd done so with many men and women before. He'd done it more than once with the same person because he liked sex and liked fun, so why keep himself from having fun with someone if they both wanted it?

But this was different. His body flamed with heat. His chest felt tight, but not in a way that he wasn't okay with. To Wes this was a big deal, and that made it a big deal for Braden, too. Regardless if the only reason was the shitty weather, the man wouldn't have asked him to stay before. Or if he had, he wouldn't have wanted it. Maybe it made him a cocky bastard, because he knew that even if it scared the fuck out of Wes, he wanted it.

He also wanted to be sure, though, too, which was the reason for his confirmation.

Wes finally nodded. "I know. I'm still asking you to stay. I don't know what it means, though."

Me, either... Though, that wasn't completely true. Something about the man got to him. He'd crawled under Braden's skin, and Braden found he wanted to keep him there.

"You can't sleep with me. I don't want to confuse Jess, but...You can have Chelle's room..."

Braden slid his hand down Wes's leg and then circled his wrist. Wes didn't even sleep in that room, though he should. "Shut the fuck up and come here." He pulled and Wes came easily. If he hadn't wanted to, Braden knew he wouldn't, but he collapsed next to him on the couch. "I'm not sleeping in your sister's room, and I might be a little dense with some things, but I definitely know it wouldn't be cool to have Jessie wake up to us in bed together." He wrapped an arm around Wes, pretty sure he was about to stick his foot in his mouth again but not willing to stop. "Though if I'm being honest, I think she knows more than the two of us. Or at least she's questioning something we won't admit. She asked me if I'm your boyfriend, ya know."

He felt Wes stiffen a little but he didn't pull away. Maybe he was blowing shit out of proportion here. Maybe he shouldn't really want to consider them together. It wasn't like he'd never had fuck buddies before, and he'd only ever had one real boyfriend, but if he had to choose, he'd say this felt more like the second option.

"Braden—"

"Shit. You're using your *shut the fuck up, Braden* voice. And here I thought I was doing better about opening my big mouth."

Wes chuckled, put his hand over Braden's jean-covered thigh, and squeezed. "Who the fuck are you?" He dropped his head against the back of the couch and looked up at the ceiling.

"I'm the guy who likes spending every Wednesday with your niece. The guy who likes fucking you but likes making you laugh just as much. I mean, you have to admit I'm good at it. The fucking and the laughing, I mean. I'm also the guy who screws up a lot, has a big mouth, is conceited as hell, pisses people off, and forgets to pay at least one bill a month. Jesus, how hard should it be to remember? It's not like they change every month, but I always forget. Guess you can say I'm the guy who's a little irresponsible, too."

Wes shook his head but smiled too. Still resting it on the back of the couch, he rolled his head to the side so he was looking at

Braden. Fuck, he wanted his mouth. Wanted it so much his whole body ached.

"You're crazy."

"Yep.."

"You cuss too much around kids, too."

"Hey! I'm getting better at that!"

Again, Wes's hand squeezed his leg. "You're pushy, and act like a kid most of the time."

"All true."

Wes sighed, then leaned against Braden. His heart went fucking crazy in a way it never had before. Going off instinct, he reached over and turned off the lamp, thinking sometimes things were easier when you didn't have to look at a person.

Wes pulled at the blanket, his feet joining Braden's on the coffee table. "You're the guy who's good as hell with my niece. The guy who would help out a friend because it's the right thing to do. And I'll admit you're right. You're the guy who's good at both fucking me and making me laugh."

The only sound filling the room was Wes's breath because Braden held his, not really sure why but doing it anyway.

"I haven't let myself give a shit about anyone besides my family for a long time, Braden but you're here…pushing your way in."

Braden felt him shake his head.

He knew exactly what Wes was saying. He cared. He could try and disguise it as Braden pushing his way in, but the end result was the same. He cared.

"Thank you. You take care of her like she's your own. That means a lot to me."

"She's a cool kid. I love spending time with her." And he did. He'd never really put any thought into having kids, but if he did, he'd love a little girl like Jessie.

Wes pulled at the blanket, covering them both up. Maybe the moment was perfect as it was. Maybe Braden should keep his mouth shut and let them be. Wes would go to his room soon, and they could keep shit the way it was, but that wasn't Braden. Nothing ventured, nothing gained. He'd always lived his life like that. It's why he moved a lot and explored, willing to try anything out. There was always something to gain by taking chances.

"Who are you, Wesley? You know who I am. Don't you think it's time you shared yourself with me, too?"

***

Wes had no idea what he was doing—what they were doing. It felt as though there was an elastic band between the two of them. The harder Wes tried to pull away from Braden, the tougher the resistance made it. He should just loosen up and let them be pulled together, because it was so much fucking easier than fighting that resistance. Though he guessed it really wasn't easier, but the urge to try stretched the band thinner and thinner.

It was more than just how he helped with Jessie. It was the coffee, and bowling and seeing them tonight. Seeing how much his niece loved and trusted Braden, and how much he thought Braden might love her, too.

It was also in the laughter, because Braden made him feel light in a way he wasn't sure he'd ever felt. The way he looked at Wes and the way he stuck around made him want to believe Braden really *wanted* to be with him. *Like he wouldn't leave...*

"Aren't you only supposed to be interested in fucking me?" he teased, not really feeling it.

"I think it started out that way."

Leave it to Braden to be completely honest.

Braden settled into the couch more and Wes relaxed against

him. He toed out of his shoes, one of them staying on the table and another hitting the floor.

"So you used to paint but you don't anymore. You've never been with a woman. You came out to your sister. Oh, I know. Tell me why you didn't go to med school. You said you wanted to be a doctor."

The urge was there to clam up, but he was tired of that. Tonight, he wanted to take a page out of Braden's book and just *talk*. "It was too much. When Mom died, she didn't have life insurance or anything, so things were tight growing up. Chelle worked like crazy to support us. Lydia and I got jobs as soon as we could, but things were never really easy. When it came time to go to school…how could I do something that would take so many years and so much money? I had responsibilities to take care of. I wanted to be able to help her the way she'd helped us growing up, and spending eight years in school wasn't the way to do that."

"You and that big heart of yours. Pretty soon it's going to get tired of not doing anything for yourself."

"We're going to have to agree to disagree on that one."

"Of course we are. I think you like arguing with me." Braden paused and Wes found himself waiting. Waiting to see what Braden would say next. "How'd you lose your mom?" he asked.

"Car accident. She was driving home after a graveyard shift and fell asleep at the wheel."

"Shit," Braden mumbled under his breath.

"It's okay. It's been a long time. I mean, I miss her. It was hard in the beginning, especially because how it happened. All she wanted to do was take care of her kids, ya know? But Chelle was there. I was close with my sisters, and we were…well, we were happy."

"You guys are alike, then, you and Chelle. You all work hard for your family, would do whatever you could to protect them. It's a good quality to have."

Those words landed in Wes's chest. How Braden always knew the right thing to say, he didn't know. Even when it was the wrong thing…it was often right. He'd never really thought of himself like his sister or his mom before, but maybe he was. "Yeah. Yeah, I guess you're right."

Wes yawned. "I should get to bed. I had a long day, and Jessie has school in the morning."

Braden didn't let him go. "One more question first."

"Yes sir."

"Oh, I like that. I want to hear that when I'm fucking you."

A loud laugh jumped out of Wes's mouth. "I can promise you those words won't be coming out of my mouth again."

Braden sighed. "You're no fun."

"Shut up and ask your question. I'm ready for bed. If you wait much longer, I won't answer."

Braden's hand ran through Wes's hair, over and over. Wes's eyes fell closed, his body relaxed and loving the feel of Braden touching him.

"What happened to your dad?"

That was an easy one. He didn't give a shit about that bastard. "He left. Mom was at work, my sisters were gone, and I was home. Asked him to play catch with me but he couldn't because he had to run to the store. I guess once he started running, he didn't stop. Never came back."

Much like Alexander in so many ways.

"That's shitty. I'm sorry, man."

Wes shrugged, ignoring the heaviness that set into his limbs. "Don't be. What's done is done." He learned a long time ago nothing would bring his father back.

Braden's hand kept moving in his hair. "You should paint me a picture sometime, Wesley."

"Never going to happen, Roth."

"Asshole."

"You're just figuring that out?"

Braden flicked his ear.

"Ouch, damn it." But he was laughing, too.

"Fine. I'll let the painting go, but… When are you going to admit you like me?" His voice was low, filled with sleepy playfulness. Wes closed his eyes, feeling the same way.

"That's another question. You said only one more earlier. I didn't agree to answer another one."

"But you will," Braden said. Damned if he wasn't right.

"I like you, Braden," he whispered, still holding his eyes closed. "I don't know how it happened, but I do."

"I like you, too."

Wes used a page out of Braden's book and said, "I know."

But Braden didn't reply. His breathing evened out and his

hand quit moving.

Just a few minutes. Wes would give himself a few minutes before he got up and went to bed.

Chapter Nineteen

Pain shot through Braden's crotch, splintering out through his whole body, which felt like it was being cut in half.

His eyes jerked open, the word *fuck* on the tip of his tongue, but he managed to hold it back when he saw a mop of blond curls belonging to the little girl who must have jumped onto his and Wes's laps, her knee hitting the wrong spot.

As if he'd called him, Jock jumped onto his lap next and licked his face.

"Shit!" Wes scrambled to a sitting position. Braden wished like hell he could call Wes on being the one to cuss in front of her, but he was too busy dying; not just from pain, but also Jock's affection.

"You said a bad word, Uncle Wes!" Jessie screeched as Braden tried to move her from his lap.

Luckily Jessie moved for him, wrapping her arms around Wes's neck and moving closer to him. A groan/deep breath pulled from Braden's throat and Jock jumped down.

"How come you and Braden slept on the couch?" she asked.

Wes looked a little panicked, his eyes darting from Braden to Jessie. He'd think it was cute if he was sure he'd ever be able to control his body again.

"We didn't mean to. We were watching TV and fell asleep," Wes finally answered.

That was answer enough for Jessie, who jumped off Wes's lap. "I'm hungry. Can we eat? Is Braden eating here? Do I have school today?"

As soon as one of her questions passed her lips she had another one. As a kid, had he been this busy early in the morning? If so, he owed his mom a thank you.

Wes didn't answer her. Instead, he pulled his cell out of his pocket. "We're late. Come on, Jess, let's go get dressed." Obviously not needing time to wake up, he pushed to his feet.

"But I'm huuunnngggrrry. I want to eat first!" Jessie whined.

"I got breakfast. You get her clothes and stuff." Braden stood, too, leaving him and Wes face to face. His eyes were slightly red, and he needed a shave, but Braden didn't want him to. He liked the growth on his face too much.

"You don't have to."

"I know." Braden winked at him. "Now stop wasting time before you make the Squirt late for school." He ruffled Jessie's hair and she giggled.

Wes pinched the front of Braden's shirt, then rubbed his hand on Braden's abs. It shouldn't be as sexy as it was.

"Thanks." He didn't move.

Braden grinned. "You're still not going." And he was okay with that.

Wes rolled his eyes at him and said, "Come on, Jess. Let's go." When they went into the room, Braden limped to the kitchen to scramble her some eggs. Just as he scooped them onto the plate, Jessie ran to the table, wearing…hell, he wasn't sure what she was wearing. It looked like a ballerina dress, but with colorful pants and boots on underneath it. He'd put her hair in a ponytail, and she wore a tiara, or whatever they were called, too.

"What's that?" he asked.

"A tutu," Wes replied.

"Why?"

"I don't know. She wanted to wear a tutu, but I didn't want her to be cold. Do you think the pants are enough to keep her warm?"

They were something alright, with blue, green, red, and purple stripes. "I don't know. I guess. It's the same as just wearing pants, but with a tutu over it. What about the crown?"

"I'm a princess!" Jessie answered for Wes. "Do I look pretty?"

"Yes." Both Braden and Wes answered in unison before laughing. Wes would have his hands full with her. The thought both made him happy and made him feel a little empty, too. She was so fun, and Braden suddenly wished he could see this routine between them more mornings than just today.

"Can I eat?" Jessie asked, and he realized he still held her plate in his hands. Braden set it in front of her, still wondering about the crazy thoughts in his head and what they meant.

"We only have about ten minutes, Jess. Where's your

backpack? I'll grab it and make you a lunch real quick."

"I don't know." Eggs fell out of her mouth as she spoke.

"You find the backpack, I got lunch," Braden found himself saying. This time Wes didn't argue, but went to the other room and started looking. Braden threw together a pb&j, grabbed some chips, a banana and a juice box, tossing them all into a brown paper bag.

"Jessie!" Wes called, a little more panic in his voice. "I can't find your backpack. Where did you put it?"

A thought popped into his head. *Shit.* "Umm... Stop looking. This one's on me. We left it in the truck yesterday. Here," Braden walked over to the coffee table and grabbed his keys. "I can take her on my way home." Wes might have asked him to stay last night, but he knew it wouldn't last.

"Do I have to wear my hat, Uncle Wes?" Jessie asked, but Wes didn't reply right away.

Wes stood next to him. "Can you hang out for a bit? I wanted—"

"Uncle Weeessss! If I wear my hat I can't wear my tiara. I want to be a princess."

"Yeah…sure. I can stay. No problem." Braden told him.

"Uncle Wes!" Jessie squealed.

Jock barked, and Braden realized he hadn't let him out. Jessie still grumbled in the background. He wondered what Wes wanted, and he wasn't sure if anything else was going on at the moment, or if they had the space for anything else to go on.

"No, you don't have to wear your hat," Wes said to her as Braden told Jock he'd be right there.

"Here," he put his keys in Wes's hand. "Take my truck. It'll be easier."

Five minutes later, Wes was easing down the driveway. Braden stood on the enclosed porch as Jock ran around looking for a place to go to the bathroom. He felt like for the first time all morning, he had time to take a breath. But another part of him, the bigger part, thought that as hectic as it was, the morning had been fun.

***

When Wes got back home, he opened the front door and immediately smelled bacon.

"I'm fucking starved!" Braden yelled from the kitchen,

obviously having heard him come in. "Get your ass in here and make the toast. I don't want the bacon or eggs to burn."

As if he didn't have a choice (though, did he want one?), Wes hung up his jacket and went straight for the kitchen. "So you *can't* do it all, huh?"

Braden stood in front of the stove, in his jeans and shirt from last night. He turned, looking at Wes over his shoulder with a mischievous smile. Dark hair trickled down his jawline, the muscles in his shoulders flexed. "Oh no. I definitely can. Just didn't want to show you up."

Wes stood in the middle of his kitchen, wondering how in the hell they got here. They'd slept together one night and never planned for it to be more than that. It wasn't like that was something he'd never done, yet now they stood in his house together, making a meal after getting Jessie ready for school.

And he wanted Braden here. That was the kicker. He hadn't wanted anyone there since Alexander. He'd thought they would spend their lives together, but then Alexander had come home one day and said he was leaving. *"Come on, Wes. If you let yourself admit it, you'd realize you don't really love me."*

But he had. He was just shit for showing it.

"Stop thinking. I don't like it when you think. Turn your brain off and make the toast." Braden's words pulled him out of the past.

"You don't like it when I think?"

"Nope. I like it when you make toast, though. That's pretty fucking cool."

Shaking his head, Wes chuckled. "You're so damn crazy."

"I like 'exciting' better."

Yeah, he did. Things were always more exciting when Braden was around. He'd never realized he liked that.

Braden finished up the bacon and eggs while Wes made the damn toast. Afterward, they sat at the table and ate together. It wasn't until Braden dropped his fork to his plate, pushing it to the center of the table, that Wes finally spoke again. "I need to start packing things away in her room." *Will you help? Will you stay?*

Of course, those questions didn't come out. That would mean he made things too easy, that he could open his mouth and say shit that needed to be said without worry about being vulnerable. Damned if Braden didn't seem to get it, though; if he didn't seem to get Wes.

Braden nodded once, pushed to his feet and said, "Let's do it."

It wasn't the first time he surprised Wes, the first time he'd shown Wes he was more than the man you saw on the surface. It wasn't the first time he thought Braden might be made up of all heart. Well, heart and a big head.

As much as his head tried to tell him he didn't want that, that he didn't want anything, for the first time years, his chest told him something different. Made him want to try because he felt good around Braden. He felt like he belonged, and that maybe the man could feel that way about Wes, too. He was honorable, and caring, and Wes couldn't see him walking away like his father had, or like Alexander had.

So when Braden smiled and cocked his head toward Chelle's room, Wes took a deep breath, reached out and looped one of his fingers with Braden's, and led the way into his sister's room, to pack away her life.

The first thing Braden did was head for the chest at the foot of her bed.

"No. Not that. Not yet. She's had that since we were kids. It was special to her." He wasn't sure why he wasn't ready for that chest yet.

"Okay."

So they started elsewhere.

They'd been at it for about two hours when Braden opened the drawer by her bed and pulled out a stack of photo albums. Wes's palms itched to grab them. His mouth opened and closed, wanting to tell Braden to put them away, that he'd deal with them later, but he did neither.

"Can I?" Braden held one up. When Wes nodded, he sat on Chelle's bed. "Sit with me."

Wes found himself getting off the floor where he sat and going back down next to Braden. He opened the first page, and Wes groaned at the picture.

"Didn't like clothes much as a kid, huh? Maybe we can adopt that attitude now." Braden nudged him with his elbow as they looked at a picture of Wes running naked when he was about two.

"Chelle said Mom used to go crazy. She'd dress me, and five minutes later I'd come out of my room having stripped everything off. Mom would have to chase me around to put clothes on me again, but I'd take them off again."

The memory made him smile.

Braden turned another page. There were lake trips and snowmen, and pictures of him or his sisters lying on the couch when they were sick.

When they got to a page with Wes from high school wearing his baseball uniform, Braden said, "Holy fuck, Wesley. You were hot."

He turned to look at his lover, whose face was only inches from his own. "You sound shocked."

"Usually when people are hot as an adult, they were funny looking as a kid—braces, long limbs, screwed up hair."

"What the fuck are you talking about?" Wes hit his shoulder with Braden's.

"It's true. Me? I wasn't nearly as hot at seventeen as I am now. The hot ones were all assholes, and they grow up to look like shit. The ones who hadn't grown into themselves yet are sexy as hell as adults."

The grin pulling Braden's lips told Wes he was joking. Plus, he had no doubt that Braden was sexy when he was younger, and had probably had all the girls and guys lusting after him. He would have been one of the nice guys, too.

"So I'm different, huh?" Wes teased. "I'm a novelty? The rare person who was hot as a teenager and is good looking as an adult?"

Braden nodded. "Except this." He brushed his thumb through the hair on Wes's chin. "Teenage Wes is missing this, and it definitely ups the hotness factor."

Wes pretended to bite at Braden's finger but he jerked it back.

"I have no doubt you were good-looking when you were younger. Wait… Did you bring all that up just so I'd give you a compliment?"

Braden clutched his heart. "I'm offended. I can't believe you think I'd do such a thing." But then he pointed to the picture album and sobered up. "Keep looking with me. Tell me stories from when you were a kid."

Braden's words made Wes's heart thump louder, made it swell in a way he hadn't thought possible. "What do you want to know?"

"Whatever you want to tell me."

So they sat there for the next hour and a half going through album after album. Braden asked questions and Wes told him stories. They laughed and talked, and the longer he looked, the more he realized how truly happy he'd been as a kid. How much he'd been loved by his mom, Chelle, and Lydia. And how much he'd at least thought he was loved by his dad, before he left.

And it helped.

Chapter Twenty

When they got through the last photo album, Wes held them on his lap. For once Braden didn't speak, waiting to see what Wes would have to say—giving him a chance to work through whatever was going around in his head.

He smiled when Wes leaned over and bumped his arm. "Thanks, Roth."

"No problem, Wesley."

Wes let out a deep breath. "I should move into this room. It makes more sense for me to be in this room."

"There's a lot more space." There was hardly enough area for the two of them to move around in Wes's current room. Not that it should matter if he could fit there or not.

"Maybe after Christmas. I'll finish getting things put away and slowly move in here." He paused, and Braden instinctively knew to keep his big mouth shut, knew that something important was coming.

"That offer still stand for Christmas?" Wes finally asked.

He drummed his thumb on his leg to keep himself busy, to give the electric currents running through him an outlet. He really fucking wanted to take Wes home. He hadn't realized how much until this second. "Always."

"I'm going to talk to Jess. I don't want her to feel like I'm taking her away from her family for the holiday, but if she wants to go, we'll go."

The drumming suddenly wasn't enough. He needed more. More movement, more touching, more *something*. When Wes turned to look at him, Braden reached over, holding Wes's chin between his first finger and thumb. "Don't ever shave this. I like it." He rubbed the rough hair beneath his fingers. Then he leaned forward and took Wes's mouth. It wasn't a rough, needy kiss, but slow, teasing, and making that urge for *more* knock into him again.

Braden let his hand drift down to hold the back of Wes's neck as he deepened the kiss, let his tongue have every part of Wes's mouth. The man matched him, his tongue demanding entrance as well, a gentle battle of lips, mouths and tongues. "How much time do we have until we have to pick up the Squirt?" he asked.

"Little over an hour."

"Shit. That means we'll have to rush."

Wes smiled against his mouth. "In over an hour?"

"Oh yeah." Reluctantly, Braden pulled back and nodded toward the door. "Shower with me, Wesley."

Suddenly it was like neither of them could get there quick enough. Wes tossed the albums to the bed and shoved to his feet. They were both moving out the door, through the house and down the hall with quick feet and laughter.

Braden stumbled into Wes when they got into the bathroom, almost making him fall. Their mouths meshed together in a mixture of kisses and laughing.

"You want me." Braden ripped his shirt over his head.

"And you're always trying to make me admit to shit." Wes's shirt was gone, then he pulled out of his pants.

Braden's almost hard cock ached at the site of his firm ass, two globes he wanted to sink his teeth into and his dick between.

"Hurry up!"

"What are you talking about? I'm naked. Stop talking and take your clothes off."

Wes reached into the shower and turned it on. Braden made quick work of his pants, pulling a rubber out of his wallet before getting rid of them.

Wrapping his arm around Wes, Braden leaned down a little and let his mouth slam down on his. They almost tripped again climbing into the shower, but Wes kept them up. As soon as they were in the small stall, Braden dropped down.

"Fuck." Wes ran a hand through Braden's hair, already looking blissed-out and Braden had yet to touch him.

He planned to remedy that. Now.

"Mmm. I don't know what I want more, your cock or your ass. Oh, I know." He licked his tongue down Wes's thick shaft. "Eenie." Then he pushed Wes so he stood sideways and Braden could reach his ass. He bit into the closest cheek. "Meenie." Wrapped a hand around his shaft. "Miney." Then turned him all the way around, pushed him so Wes's chest leaned against the shower wall. "Moe." He traced Wes's crack with his tongue.

"*Fuck*..." Wes shivered, and Braden smiled.

"You like that? I do, too." Water rained down on them as Braden lapped at Wes's hole. Wes moaned, moving his ass closer to Braden's hungry mouth. Braden let his tongue swirl around Wes's pucker, his nails squeezing into Wes's right cheek. Jesus, he wasn't sure he'd ever get tired of this. He loved the feel of Wes against him. The sounds he made. Being the one to bring him pleasure.

Braden pushed a finger into his tight hole, using his other hand to thread between Wes's legs to wrap around his dick.

Wes's hips rocked forward and backward, fucking himself on Braden's finger and also thrusting into his hand. "Holy shit." Wes dropped his forehead against the wall of the shower. "Keep that up and I'm going to come."

Braden pushed in deeper, twisting his finger. "That's the point, baby."

"But I want you to fuck me. Wanna come while you're fucking me." He looked down, over his shoulder at Braden, and damned if his breath didn't fucking catch. Seeing his taut, lithe body as water poured down it, that goatee that drove him fucking crazy, the need in his eyes and the smile that Braden was starting to consider *his*. The one he only saw when Wes looked at him. He wanted to keep it there.

"Well, since you asked nicely." Braden winked and pushed to his feet. He grabbed the condom from the edge of the tub, opened it and rolled it down his shaft. The water was their lube and the ass play already prepared Wes. Braden wrapped his arms around Wes's stomach, lined his chest up to the man's back, and pushed inside. His cock jerked, his balls burned with the need to come, surrounded by all that tight heat.

"You're not moving," Wes groaned.

"You want this over before it starts?"

"Come on, Roth. You're better than that."

Yeah, he was. Or he'd make himself be. He pulled out and thrust forward again. He let go of Wes's waist, pulling the man's hands over his head and threading their fingers together from behind as he made love to him. It wasn't just fucking right now.

Their bodies slapped together. The water started to turn cold, but it wasn't enough to put out their fires. He kissed Wes's neck, let go of one hand when the man obviously wanted to jerk himself off. But Braden wanted that, too, so he twined their fingers together so they could both jack Wes.

It went quickly after that. As soon as Wes's muscles clamped around him, a curse pulled from Wes's throat and he came in their hands. Braden shot, too, his orgasm drowning him in a series of waves.

Wes leaned against the shower wall, his forehead against it and Braden's against the back of his head, as they came down from their high.

"Was that good enough?" Braden finally asked with a laugh.

"Yeah…yeah, it was."

***

Wes sat at the kitchen table with Jessie that evening. They'd gotten pizza because it was her favorite, and were drinking hot chocolate while playing *Memory*.

His stomach was in knots, which he had to admit was a little ridiculous. He was nervous about talking to Jessie about this. The last thing he wanted was to screw up with her, to do the wrong thing or to make her feel like he was taking more away from her than she already lost. But then…she liked Braden, too. She would love to spend a holiday with him. The idea of getting away made his chest feel light.

But then those damn nerves hit again because this was big. He'd never met a man's family except for Alexander, and he hadn't planned to do it again.

"Hey, Jess? What would you think of going with Braden for a few days over Christmas?"

She looked up at him. "With you?"

"Of course, sweetheart. I'll be there, too. And Braden's family. He has lots of nieces and nephews you could play with."

Her little eyes lit up at that. "But what about Santa? Will he know where I am?"

Ah, of course. It always came back to Santa, didn't it? "Of course. He knows everything."

"Will aunt Lydia come, too?" she asked. Wes shook his head.

"No. She'll stay here. And if you want, we'll stay here, too. It's all up to you."

"I wanna go with Braden!"

Was it possible to feel excitement and dread at the same time? Her statement worried him but also made him thankful...because he wanted to go with Braden, too. *Please let me be doing the right thing.* Was it smart to get so entwined with a man right now? To let Jessie spend more time with him when she obviously loved him? What if they stopped whatever this was they were doing? What if it hurt her?

"Uncle Wes, do you love Braden? I love Eric."

Wes almost swallowed his tongue. How did he answer this? "Braden is a good friend to us. He helps us out a lot and I like him. You like him, too, right?"

She nodded and took a bite of her food. "Is he your boyfriend? Are you gonna get married?"

The weight in his gut doubled. He thought about everything Braden had done for them. About helping him go through Chelle's room and his promise to help again. The shower and the press of Braden's lips to his forehead when he'd left. Holy shit, Braden was pretty much his boyfriend…and he was strangely okay with that.

He ignored the marriage part, because how could you explain to a four-year-old that the world was a fucked up place and marriage wasn't something that was equal? "I don't know what Braden is to me, kiddo."

"Do you like him?"

The words weren't as sticky in his mouth as he'd thought they would be. "I do."

"He makes you laugh. I like it when you laugh." Jessie got up and climbed on his lap. Wes held onto her, feeling like he had a mini-version of his sister in his arms.

"I like laughing, too."

"I wanna go. Can we go with Braden?"

He squeezed her tighter. "Let's do it." He wanted nothing more.

Chapter Twenty-One

Braden just finished zipping his suitcase when his phone rang. His first instinct was to ignore it, that way if it was Wes calling to cancel, he couldn't. It wasn't as if he'd let the man change his mind, anyway, so he went ahead and pulled the cell out of his pocket to see that it was Cooper.

"Hey, man. What's up?" Braden asked when he answered.

"Sitting here with two dogs running around me. My boyfriend decided we both needed pets for Christmas."

"Don't pretend you don't like it," Braden said, and heard Noah saying something similar in the background.

He didn't know why, but that made him smile. Braden sat

down on his bed and asked, "You're really happy?" He knew the answer to the question before he'd asked.

"Of course," Cooper replied.

"Yeah, I know. Dumb question. It's just, I can't help but think about you *before*. It's not that I've never been in a relationship like you hadn't. You not only committed to someone for the first time, but it was another man. It's just…" What was he trying to say?

"You're serious about Wes. What are you asking? If I miss the single life?"

No, he didn't think so…was he? Again, he'd been in monogamous relationships before. *Relationships I knew wouldn't last forever…* Yet, with Wes, he wasn't sure he could say the same thing.

"I don't, if that's what you're asking," Coop said. "I don't want anyone but him. What's there to miss when I have what I want?"

Braden nodded as though Cooper could see him. "I don't know what I'm thinking or why I asked that."

"Well, you didn't technically ask, and it's because you're thinking about getting serious with someone for the first time. If you haven't already."

"Shut up," Braden teased. "We've had too many of these heart to hearts lately. What's up? What are you guys doing for Christmas?"

"Not much. Hanging out with the dogs, I guess. Noah wants to try and cook a turkey. Neither of us have ever done it before. Should be a good time."

Braden chuckled.

"How's shit at work? Fred still being a bastard?"

Was Fred ever not a bastard? "He's being himself, which is a yes. It doesn't bother me, though. He can fuck off for all I care. He avoids me and I avoid him."

"He'll be doing that with both of us when I go back next month. Good thing I don't give a shit, either."

Braden pushed to his feet, grabbed his bag, and headed for the living room. "You guys want to come to my parents? They'll love it."

"Nah, that's okay. You need the time with your man," Cooper teased him. The bastard.

"Your loss. I need to get my ass off the phone, though. I gotta grab Wes and Jessie so we can get on the road." As soon as he opened the front door, Jock ran out with him.

"Have fun. Drive safe. Merry Christmas."

"You, too."

Braden was about to hang up when Cooper said, "Hey. You won't regret it if you go there."

Braden opened his truck and put his bag in. Jock jumped into the backseat and laid down with a thump that matched the one hitting Braden's gut. He wasn't so worried about himself. Not really. It was Wes he worried about. Wes he wasn't sure would ever take that next step.

***

Jessie talked enough for both herself and Wes as they drove to Braden's family's house. He guessed that was a good thing, because he wasn't sure what he would say, anyway. It hadn't been like this for the past two weeks since he'd decided to go, but then, they'd both been busy. He'd covered some extra shifts at the hospital because of time off, which they usually didn't give around the holidays.

They were together on Wednesdays, when Braden stayed for dinner now, but most of the past two weeks Wes had spent with Jessie because of Christmas break. When Braden hung out with them, they had too much fun to really let Wes's mind wander.

This was different. This was the enclosed space of Braden's truck as they drove to spend five days with Braden's family.

He was being a fucking pussy.

"How many kids is there?" Jessie asked for the third time.

"Six," Braden said as Wes replied, "Are. How many kids *are* there."

They both ignored him and Braden continued talking. "But my sister is pregnant. She's due next month. Maybe the baby will come early and there will be seven before we leave. Plus you, Squirt. That would be eight of you guys."

Jessie giggled in the backseat and stroked Jock's head as it lay in her lap.

They spoke off and on for the rest of the ride, and before he knew it, Braden pulled off the road and onto a long driveway lined with trees on either side. Snow covered the ground and colored trees as they slowly made their way toward the house. It wasn't long until the trees opened up to a huge chunk of snow-covered land with a large, ranch-style home with red shutters.

"My parents built her from the ground up. Drew their own

plans and everything." Braden pulled up in front of the house and killed the engine.

"It's incredible," Wes told him, and it really was. It was large without being overdone. Homey and somehow modern, but also like it had been around for years.

"Thanks." Wes turned to Braden when he spoke, and the man winked at him before looking into the cab. "There's tons of space for you and Jock to play here. There's an old fort I built when I was a kid. I'll show it to you."

"Yay!" Jessie bounced in the seat.

Despite the awkwardness Wes felt, he reached over and squeezed Braden's leg, hoping Braden knew it meant he appreciated all he did. He appreciated how good he was with Jessie, the fact that he invited them out here in the first place and also dealt with Wes's moodiness.

When Braden nodded, the blood pushed through Wes's body more swiftly, and somehow he relaxed slightly. Braden got what he couldn't say.

"Let's go, Squirt," Braden said to Jessie, and they all climbed out of the truck. She immediately started to play with Jock. Wes wasn't surprised when Braden walked over to his side of the truck. "We're good, Wesley. No biggie. Just try and have fun, yeah?"

Before Wes had a chance to reply, a woman's voice yelled, "Braden Roth, you get your butt up here right now and give your mama a hug!"

With a wink and a smile, Braden looked at Wes and said, "It's show time."

Braden nodded toward the house. The gleam in his eyes told Wes he was up to something. Jessie was with Jock about halfway between the house and where they stood. "Race us to the house, Jess!" he called, and she immediately started running. Braden did, too, though he wasn't sure he could call what either of them were doing actual running because of the snow and their clothes. Still, one foot in front of the other, Wes found himself chasing after them. They both slowed down, letting Jessie win, but the second she hit the steps, they both went faster, obviously neither wanting the other to win.

"Yay!" Jessie shouted when they both slid to a stop in front of the porch at the same time.

"Tie," Braden said.

"Yeah, but you started before me," Wes argued, watching the white plumps of heat in the air when he spoke.

"Oh, God. Don't tell me you're as competitive as he is." The woman took a step toward them.

"Who are you?" Jessie asked.

"Jess, don't—" Wes began, but Braden's mom cut him off. "It's okay."

She kneeled down, reminding him of Braden. "I'm Emmy, Braden's mom. Let me guess…you're Jessie? Braden said you were only four, but you're such a big girl. Are you sure you aren't six?"

"Hi," Jess whispered, and then wrapped her arms around Wes's leg and buried her face into it.

"You don't need to be shy with my mom, Squirt. She's pretty much just a big kid herself," Braden laughed.

"Like you?" both Emmy and Wes said at the same time.

"Oh, I like you." Emmy pushed to her feet. "And you must be Wes. Braden talks about you all the time." She winked at Wes. Oh yeah. He and his mom were a lot alike.

"Don't tell him shit like that, Ma. He has a big head. We don't want to make it bigger."

"You said a bad word!" Jessie told him, and Braden grabbed her.

"None of that." He swooped her over his shoulder like a sack of potatoes.

Wes couldn't stop himself from watching him. Watching Jessie and Braden laugh. And damn, if he didn't like what he saw. When he felt a soft hand on his arm, he turned to look at Emmy, who watched them, too. "It's good to meet you, Wes," she said, still watching Braden. "We're happy to have you here."

He nodded. "I'm happy to be here, too."

Chapter Twenty-Two

Wes was feeling overwhelmed. It only took one look for Braden to realize that. Not that he could blame him. He knew his family could be a lot. There were not only a lot of them, but they were also all just like him. It was enough to stress anyone out, but that's the last thing he wanted from Wes out of this trip. For once, he wanted him to just be able to let go. To relax and enjoy himself completely.

Braden watched as he sat on the couch with his dad and sister Yvonne, who were both obviously on different sides of whatever issue they were talking about, leaving Wes in the middle. His sister's hands were flying because she couldn't talk without using them, and his dad was shaking his head, giving that Roth-you-don't-know-what-the-hell-you're-talking-about look. Wes's eyes kept darting back and forth between the two of them.

Each time Wes opened his mouth to speak, either Braden's dad or sister would start yapping again and cut him off.

"Go save that boy, Braden." His mom sat on the arm of his chair.

"It's cute to watch, though. He's totally out of his element here, but I think he's having a good time, too."

"His family isn't close?" she asked.

"No." He shook his head. "They are, but there's never been a lot of them. His dad left when he was young, and then he lost his mom a few years later. His sister raised them, and now she's gone, too." The words hollowed him out a little. Yes, he'd always known they were true, but his gut ached for Wes. He wanted him to have everything.

"That's sad. He looks like he's going to run at any second, though. Go save him before he never wants to come back. You know how your dad and sister can get."

Braden looked into the family room to see Jessie playing a video game with one of his nephews. "You'll watch Jess?"

The corners of his mom's eyes wrinkled like she was looking

at him for the first time. Braden was about to ask her why when she said, "That's a dumb question. Of course I will."

Braden stood and kissed her on the forehead. "Thanks, Ma." He walked over to where Wes sat. The second Wes saw him, his features relaxed. "I need to show you something real quick."

Wes pushed to his feet. Yvonne and his dad said bye and then got right back into their argument. Wes followed Braden to the front door and stopped when Braden said, "Go outside with me, Wesley."

"What about Jessie?"

"She's having fun. She probably won't even notice we're gone. And if she does, Mom will watch her. She'll call me if Jessie needs us—you. If she needs you." He wanted that, he realized. Wanted them to officially be an *us*. Wanted to be there for Jessie, too. He wasn't sure to what extent, but he knew it was there.

Braden grabbed Wes's jacket from the closet and tossed it to him. Wes caught it and Braden grabbed his own. Once they each were clothed in coats, beanies, and gloves, he opened the door for Wes, who stepped out.

"Where are we going?" he asked.

"Not far. You looked like you were ready to bolt on my sister and dad, so I figured you needed a break. Plus, I really want to show you something."

They were silent as they walked through the dark, around the backside of the house, and up the small hill. The air around them was cold as hell, but he ignored it. A few minutes later, they made it to the top of the hill and Wes froze in his tracks. Braden couldn't help but smile. He wrapped his arms around Wes's waist from behind as they looked down at the lights of the city below. At the oversized Christmas tree in the center of it, lit up with different colors, and the snow on top of businesses.

"Jesus, man. It looks like a postcard or something," Wes whispered.

"It's beautiful, isn't it? I used to sneak out here at night sometimes when I was younger. I'd spend half the night looking at it…well, I don't really know why. But yeah, I always liked it." Leaning forward, Braden rested his chin on Wes's shoulder. "Wanted you to see it."

He felt Wes stiffen a little, but then his body relaxed. He laid his arms over Braden's, which were still around him. "Aww, are you a closet romantic, Braden?" he teased.

"Do you want me to be?" Braden countered.

It took Wes a minute to reply. "I don't like the fact that I'm pretty sure I'd like you no matter how you are."

His body suddenly wasn't cold anymore. In this moment, he felt like nothing could harm him. "You say shit like that to me, Wesley, and you're going to make me want to claim you."

"I'm sure you tell all the guys…and girls that." There was a forced playfulness to his voice that Braden knew he tried to put there.

"Whatever you have to tell yourself." He kissed Wes's neck. The man turned around immediately, his mouth coming down on Braden's this time. His gloved hands held the sides of Braden's face as Braden's arms wrapped around his waist again. It was a slow, sensual assault, a slow dance of tongues, probing then pulling back for the other to lead. He tasted mint, and wondered if Wes had chewed gum or brushed his teeth after dinner. He felt the warmth of man, making the cold evaporate.

Braden sucked Wes's lip into his mouth then gently bit it. When he tried to pull back, Wes nipped at him. "Come back here," he whispered, and then they were kissing again. He let his hand slide down to cup Wes's ass, swallowed the moan that pulled from Wes's throat.

He reveled at the feel of Wes's facial hair against his own. His cock got hard even though he knew he wouldn't get to use it tonight. Wes would be in Braden's old room with Jessie, and Braden was sleeping on the futon in the office. He wouldn't get to use it on this trip at all unless he was alone. But this right here? For the first time in his life, this was enough.

***

The house was even more hectic the next morning than it had been the night before. Emmy was in the kitchen making a huge breakfast. There was a table full of kids drinking hot chocolate and pretty much yelling over each other so they could all speak at the same time—Jessie right in the middle of them. She fell right in with Braden's family, like she'd always belonged. That had a lot to do with the Roth clan. He was pretty sure they were some of the most incredible people out there and that they'd make anyone feel at home—like they belonged.

The way Braden does with me…? Wes pushed those thoughts aside.

It was noon before everyone was dressed, fed and ready to leave. Apparently it was a Roth family tradition to go into the woods and cut down their own tree on Christmas eve.

"Why do you do it so late?" Wes asked as they drove.

"My parents have always done it that way. They say the tree should be special, and it should be about Christmas. If it's up for weeks ahead of time, then it doesn't feel new, like something special for that specific day." He chuckled. "I don't know. It's something Mom came up with when we were kids, and Dad always says a happy wife makes a happy life."

Those words soured Wes's stomach, though he wasn't sure why until Braden said, "Though, I like 'A happy spouse makes a happy house' better."

The fact that his words helped made Wes feel like an idiot. "You're cheesy."

"You like me that way."

He did.

A little while later, the vehicles were parked and the army that was Braden's family stomped through the trees, looking for the perfect one. It wasn't a short walk, and no one could seem to agree on which one they wanted.

"I'm tired, Uncle Wes." Jessie tugged on his arm. He picked her up and swung her onto his back.

"I got you, kiddo." He paused when Braden stepped up to them and ran a hand down Jessie's back. When he did, she relaxed against Wes, resting her head on his shoulder.

"Ma, Dad. If we don't pick one soon, we have to go. Jess is getting tired," Braden called to his family.

Damned if what Braden said didn't hit him in the chest. "Thanks. We're good, though. I don't want to ruin the day for everyone."

"They can stay if they haven't decided. If we need to go back, we need to go back. She's more important than picking the perfect tree."

Who the fuck was this guy? How many times had Braden said the wrong thing, but, when it counted, always said the right thing? He didn't know if he realized that. Didn't know if he realized that the more Wes was around him, the more he feared he wouldn't ever want to be without him. That he made Wes think and feel shit he never thought he would again.

No, things he hadn't felt before.

"Hey." Wes grabbed Braden's arm when he tried to walk away. "Thanks."

Braden just winked at him. "I'll put it on your 'I owe you' list."

Again, it was the perfect thing to say. The asshole.

Chapter Twenty-Three

They'd picked an eight-foot tree. Braden and his brother Evan put it in the stand and watered it while their mom and sisters made dinner. They were going easy tonight because they were all pretty exhausted after a long day.

They sat around the living room, the kids on the floor around the coffee table, eating grilled cheese sandwiches and tomato soup.

"'Member when Braden made us grilled cheese?" Jessie asked Wes. Braden wasn't sure if she was too tired to remember the "R" in Remember, or if she always said it that way.

"I do," Wes told her.

"Braden's were better," she replied.

"Jessie!" Wes's eyes darted around the room, obviously embarrassed.

"Hey. Can't blame her for speaking the truth." Braden smiled, and everyone else laughed, including Emmy and Lizzy.

"That's okay, because I taught him how to cook." Emmy gave Jessie a thumbs-up. He couldn't love his mom more. Any of his family, really. They took Jessie and Wes in without question, though he knew they all wondered what was going on between them. Braden wondered, too. And regardless of the fact that none of them ever really understood his attraction to both men and women, they never gave him a hard time about it, either.

"Can we decorate the tree now?" Billy asked. His sister had named the little boy after their father.

"We sure as hell can!" Braden and his dad both shot to their feet.

"As soon as everyone puts their dishes away," his mom added. So they did. The kids raced to the kitchen, cleaning up without whining probably for the first time in their lives. They'd already pulled the boxes out, and his dad had added the lights, so once the dishes were gone, kids ripped into containers and started hanging decorations on the bottom half of the tree.

Jessie jumped right in as Braden knew she would, but Wes

stood back a little, the way Braden knew he would do as well.

"Get your ass up here and help," Braden told him. Jessie was too busy decorating to call him on his language. "If we don't help we're going to have a seriously lopsided tree. Most of the decorators are shrimps, if you didn't notice."

Wes shook his head with a smile on his face. It was that smile he gave when he wasn't sure what to do with Braden, but that he enjoyed him, too. It was Braden's favorite of his grins.

Wes beside him, they all decorated the tree. They turned out the living room lights and watched all the reds, greens, blues and whites glow. As they talked, Braden kept his eyes on Wes, who sat on the floor with Jessie's head in his lap. Wes stroked her curls, which just popped back up as soon as his hand left them. Her little eyes kept drooping closed, but each time they did, she jerked them open again.

She was such a cool little kid. He'd never given much thought of having kids of his own. His family had enough of them if he never did, but looking at her…he couldn't imagine his life without her. His eyes met Wes's, who Braden hadn't realized had been watching him.

Braden opened his mouth to say something—what, he didn't know—when Wes said, "I'm going to put her to bed."

"No. I don't wanna go to bed." Jessie started crying.

"You're sleepy, kiddo, and it's getting late. We need to go to bed so Santa can come." Wes stood her up, pushed to his feet and then picked her up.

Braden was surprised when Jessie started crying louder. He stood, too, not really sure why. She was Wes's niece. He had this under control. He didn't need Braden. "I'll take care of the stuff."

Wes nodded, and Braden knew he got that he'd put Jessie's Santa gifts out.

"Night, everyone." Wes's voice was hardly heard over Jessie's crying. Wes looked a little freaked out, too, his eyes wide and his body stiff, as though he wasn't sure what was going on with her, either.

As they went, Braden's dad stepped up beside him. "Told you it was more than just friends."

He didn't reply. Braden didn't move from where he stood, just watched Wes disappear with Jessie. For the first time in his life, he felt left out of something he really wanted to be a part of.

***

"But Santa's not going to find me!" Jessie cried for the

millionth time. Wes sat with her in the bed, Jessie on his lap as he rocked her back and forth.

"Yes he will, kiddo. I promise." Damn it. He's screwed up. He thought it might not be a good idea to pull her away from her home and her family the first Christmas she spent without her mom, but he'd thought she would be okay with him and Braden. "You have to go to bed, though. Santa can't come if you don't go to bed."

"I want Braden," she cried. And Wes's heart broke… It meant so much to him that she loved Braden, but he was her uncle. When she needed someone, he wanted it to be him.

"Braden's with his parents right now, Jess. I'm here, though."

There were more tears. She wrapped her arms around him tightly. "I want Braden. Santa won't come cuz I can't sleep. I want you and Braden."

Wes exhaled a deep breath. She wanted him, too. She wanted them both. Red flags flew up. Wes would always be there for her, but Braden didn't have to be.

"I miss Mommy…" she whispered. The words were a knife through his chest. He got it now. She didn't want to be alone. She wanted to keep people she loved close to her. She wanted him and Braden. To her, they were her family. They were who she had.

"I miss her, too, kiddo." Wes grabbed his cell off the nightstand. He didn't let himself think about what this meant for him. The step he was taking, or the fact that this made it more real. All he knew was Jessie needed them, and he'd do anything to give her what she needed.

And he knew Braden would, too.

Jessie needs you, he texted. A minute later, there was a knock at the bedroom door.

"That's Braden," he told her. "I'm going to set you down and let him in." He knew it was a precaution he didn't need to take, that Braden wouldn't think twice to give them what they needed. *Her. Give her what she needs, I mean.*

He opened the door and peeked his head out. "She's having a hard time. She misses her mom. She wants…"

"Let me in, Wesley. You know I won't walk away."

Wes opened the door and Jessie ran to him. Braden picked her up and held her. "Santa won't find me."

"He knows you're here, Squirt. I already talked to him. He wanted to come, but I told him you were still awake. He said he'll be back in about an hour, but we have to be sleeping by then."

"Can you sleep with us, too, Uncle Braden?" Wes and Braden both froze at her words—at the name she called him. Braden's eyes sought his, a pleading that Wes had never seen from him. He gave the man a single nod.

"Yeah. Of course." He laid Jessie on the bed. Wes had already gotten her into her pajamas, and he was in sweats and a T-shirt. Braden kicked out of his shoes as Wes covered Jessie with the blanket.

"Do you want to go change first?" Wes asked him, but Braden just shook his head. No hesitation, he climbed into the queen-sized bed in his jeans and shirt, next to Jessie. Wes inhaled a deep breath, and lay on the other side of her. She was the only one under the blankets. He knew they'd get cold, but it didn't matter. Reaching over, Wes clicked the light on the table. The room went dark except for a light shining through the window from outside. A porch light, maybe, but it was enough that he could make out both their facial features.

"Does Mommy get presents where she is?" Jessie asked.

"Yeah, she does," Wes replied, his heart pulling from his chest. He rolled to his left side, looking at her. Braden laid on his right side, facing the middle of the bed, too.

"Night, Uncle Wes. I love you."

He kissed her forehead. "Good night, baby girl. I love you, too."

"Night, Uncle Braden. I love you."

Wes held his breath at Jessie's words, but not Braden. True to who he was, the man who didn't hesitate, who gave anything he could to help someone, who was maybe the best man he'd ever known, opened his mouth and said, "Night, Squirt. I love you, too."

Jessie's eyes closed and she fell right to sleep. But not Wes. As he and Braden looked at each other over Jessie's sleeping body, he realized he'd lied when he texted Braden. It wasn't just Jessie who'd needed him. Wes needed him, too.

Chapter Twenty-Four

Braden awoke to the sound of whispering.

"Shh. We should let him sleep, Jess."

"I don't wanna let him sleep. It's Christmas! Santa came."

"It's early, kiddo. Just because you're an early bird," Wes told her playfully. Braden tried not to smile. "The rest of the house might not be awake yet."

"But I wanna play with him. Don't you wanna play with Uncle Braden?"

Wes was silent for a second before replying, "We can play with him later. He's still sleeping."

Braden pretended to snore loudly.

"Shh!" Jessie giggled.

"You fake." Wes pushed Braden's arm and he let his eyes pop open.

"Who can sleep with you two around?" he teased as he sat up in the bed.

Wes and Jessie did the same. Wes scratched the back of his neck, looking over at Braden through the bend in his arm. Christ, the man was sexy as hell. More than that, he made Braden's pulse speed up, made him want to smile bigger, because he could get used to waking up like this.

Braden jumped out of the bed. "Are you guys always in bed so late on Christmas? Let's go open gifts, even if we have to wake up the whole house to do it."

"Yay!" Jessie started jumping on the bed, jumped right off the edge and ran for the door. She was out it before Wes even stood.

"Hey." Wes grabbed his arm as Braden tried to walk past him. "Thanks for last night. It means a lot to me."

"Anytime. Anything. Come on." Braden slid his hand behind Wes's neck, pulling him close. "You gotta know that by now, don't you?" He wasn't sure he could deny Wes anything he needed. Wasn't sure he wanted to.

Wes didn't speak. He didn't pull away, either. His lips pressed to Braden's in a brief kiss.

"You're welcome." Braden gave him another kiss. "Plus, she's a great kid. I'm honored as hell to be 'Uncle Braden' to her."

Wes pulled away and gave him a small nod. "Come on. We better get out there before she opens everyone's gifts."

Excitement skittered through Braden. Crazy as it was, he'd always loved Christmas. He felt like a kid himself. And he couldn't wait for Wes and Jessie to see what he'd gotten them.

He heard voices as they took the stairs. Apparently everyone had made it down to the tree before he and Wes. His sister Lizzy was playing Santa. They rotated, each of them being the one to pass out gifts each year.

Jessie sat in the middle of the floor with the rest of his nieces and nephews.

"About time you got down here!" Lizzy teased. "I wasn't sure how long I could hold them off."

"Dig in," Braden chuckled as he watched Wes sit down next

to Jessie. She was already ripping into a gift before his ass hit the ground. His parents got her a doll. Wes got her a gift card for the pet store back home, where they would go pick out their own puppy. Santa brought a sled, and Braden got her a life-sized brown lab stuffed animal.

He and his siblings didn't exchange gifts, focusing on the children instead, so he was surprised when he got another gift after opening the one from his parents.

"What'd you get me, Wesley?" he winked at the man, who couldn't reply before Jessie did.

"I picked it out!"

"Oh, it's from you? Thanks, Squirt." He playfully tugged on one of her curls.

Braden ripped at the paper and smiled when he pulled out a large toy fire truck. He caught Wes's eye and the man shrugged, obviously a little embarrassed about the gift.

"Do you like it?" Jessie asked.

"Are you kidding me? I love it. Come here." She fell into his lap and he gave her a hug. He really did love the gift. It didn't matter to him that it was a toy.

She scrambled away from him as fast as she'd come, looking at the toys with the other kids. He'd hidden Wes's gift behind the tree, not sure how Wes would feel if he gave it to him in front of everyone or not. Since they gave him something, he was going for it, though.

Braden grabbed the gift. The kids were all laughing and playing still. He knew his parents were watching him, and probably his sisters, too. Shit like that didn't bother him though. Braden kneeled next to Wes. "Thanks for the truck, Wesley."

He rolled his eyes and shook his head. "Sorry. She wouldn't go for anything else."

"I don't want anything else either." He sat down and handed Wes the gift before leaning back, his hands flat on the floor behind him.

Wes paused, looking at the package and then Braden. He had to figure what was inside, and this could be one of those moments were Braden opened mouth and inserted foot, but he didn't think so. At least he hoped not.

***

Wes's fingers begged to rip into the package. A passion he'd long since thought he buried flared to life inside him again. The urge to paint, that he hadn't felt in so long, made him buzz with energy. At the same time, this felt deeply personal. This was showing a part of who he really was, who he used to be to Braden and his family.

But then, Braden had known. Braden knew more about him than anyone had in a very long time.

"You opening them or what, Wesley?" Braden teased.

"Shut up," he found himself saying as he tore the paper on the first package. Inside were a few blank canvases. He wasn't sure why but he flipped through them, as though each blank canvas would be different. They weren't, of course, until...He couldn't stop the grin on his face.

"You know what they say about assuming, don't you?" he directed at Braden.

"That you get your way?" Braden replied.

"Great. What'd he do this time?" Braden's dad, Bill, joked.

Wes looked at the corner of the last canvas, where it said, "For Braden."

"I'm forcing him to paint something for me," Braden replied for him. "Open the rest."

He opened the other package, a bag filled with oil paints and brushes. His chest swelled the whole time. He wanted this. How had he not realized he wanted to do this again?

"I hope that's all the right stuff. I didn't know what all you needed. I'm pretty sure the lady at the art store thought I was an idiot."

"Yeah, it's right." Wes set everything back in the bag. He looked over, holding Braden's eyes. This meant a lot to him. Christ, it meant more to him than he realized it would. No one else would have pushed it like this. He didn't know he would want someone to, but Braden knew.

"Thank you."

Braden shook his head. "It's not a big deal."

"Yes it is." The room was loud with laughter and chatter, but he just kept staring at Braden, kept trying to show him what this meant to him.

"You're welcome," Braden finally said with a nod.

"Who's ready for breakfast?" Emmy asked, to which everyone started talking at the same time and getting up to head for the kitchen. He stood first and held out his hand to help Braden up. As they headed toward the kitchen with everyone else, Wes kept their hands latched together.

Chapter Twenty-Five

When Jessie had asked to go outside and play with her sled a little while before, Braden told Wes he had to help his mom with a few things, which he usually did on the holidays. But he didn't have to. Still, he'd thought it a good idea to give Jessie and Wes some time alone—Wes especially. Though Jessie seemed to be doing okay today, the day couldn't be easy on either one of them. He wouldn't let himself push.

"Did your father show you the deathtrap on two wheels he has sitting in the shop?" his mom asked as Braden put the milk in the fridge.

"It's not a deathtrap, woman. It's a badass machine. Isn't it, Braden?" his father replied, before getting a swat on the arm from his mom.

"It should be illegal to say 'badass' after the age of sixty," she told him. "And don't call me 'woman.'"

Braden laughed at them both as he moved toward the dish drain to help put dishes away. He loved his parents. Knew he was damn lucky to have them.

"I have to agree with Dad on this one, Ma. It's a Harley."

"I'm not speaking to you anymore." She stirred something on the stove.

His dad laughed, plucked a glass out of Braden's hand, and said, "Wes is a good man. I like him." Then he filled his glass with water and left the kitchen.

"It really does worry me, Brady." She crossed her arms, using the nickname only his mom sometimes used. Braden nodded at her to come to him, and she did.

"He'll be okay. I don't even know if he really wants to ride it. I think he just likes saying he has it. And if he does, you know he'll be careful." Braden nudged her. "Plus, you have a few months before you have to worry about it much, anyway. I could always take it off his hands if you want."

She rolled her eyes. "What am I going to do with you Roth boys?"

Braden turned back toward the sink, packing the glasses from the drain into the cabinet next to it. As he worked he saw Wes and Jessie through the window. Wes would carry both Jess and the sled up the hill before riding back down with them again. He got this heaviness in his chest. Nothing uncomfortable, but a good kind of ache.

"You're in love with him." His mom stood beside him, their arms touching.

"Maybe." *Probably.* "How do I know?"

"Your mama tells you."

He let out a deep breath, but smiled, too.

"Sorry. Ask silly questions and you'll get a silly answer. You do, and you know you do. I see it in the way you look at him. But I think you've known for a while."

Braden stood there, still watching them. "I respect the hell out of him. He puts everyone before himself. He loves that little girl with everything he has. He makes me feel good. Making him smile makes me feel good, because he does it more with me than anyone else. I feel settled with them. Not sure I've ever felt settled in my whole life."

His mom hooked her arm through his and leaned on his

shoulder. "I'm not sure you have, either."

They both knew it wasn't because Braden wasn't happy, or hadn't always been. He'd just always been looking for something, even when he didn't know what. Maybe he did now. "Does it bother you?" he asked her after a minute of silence.

"Braden Jeffrey Roth, I can't believe you even asked me that. You know all we've ever wanted is for our kids to be happy. And it's not like we haven't known this for a very long time."

"Yeah, but you always knew there was the possibility of a woman, too. You knew I dated mostly women. It's one thing to know I like men, too, and another to know I'm *in love* with one."

"In whose book?" She hugged his arm tighter. "Not in ours, and not in yours, either. You know that, Brady. I just want you to be able to look back when you're my age and be as happy as I am. We'll love whoever can give you that, and we'll kick anyone's ass who can't."

He looked down at her. "Don't let Jess hear you talk like that."

"Would never happen. Unlike you, I know when to open my mouth and when not to."

With his other hand, Braden held her arm. Jessie and Wes

went racing down the hill again, Wes walking up it slower and slower each time. Jessie didn't look like she was going to tire at any second.

"You're right. I don't know why I asked that. I'm feeling a little out of my element, and that's never happened before. I didn't expect this." He didn't know if Wes would want it. "He has a lot he's dealing with right now. I've been known to push, Ma. I don't wanna push if he's not ready."

"You'll do the right thing. We may tease you, but when it comes down to it, you always do the right thing. It's just who you are." She patted his hand and then pulled away. "Now get dressed and go out there and help the poor boy. She's going to wear him into the ground if you don't. You guys are going to have your hands full with that girl. You mark my words." She winked at him, and Braden wondered if she thought Wes might love him, too.

"Thanks, Ma." Braden didn't hesitate. He went straight for his jacket and boots, hoping his mom was right. Hoping he'd do the right thing, and that Wes would give him some kind of sign as to when to do it.

***

Wes watched as Braden and Jock traipsed up the hill with Jessie for the hundredth time. They'd been taking turns ever since

Braden came out a little while before. Just like Wes did, he struggled to carry her in her ten pounds of snow gear, plus the sled up the hill; only Braden had Jock trying to play with him, too.

He watched as Braden tripped, managing to catch himself before he went down. Wes laughed. "Need some help up there?" he called.

"Shut up!"

Wes laughed again. "I'll help if you ask real nicely."

"Shut up!" Braden called down again as he heard Jessie scolding him because "shut up" wasn't nice.

Wes couldn't take his eyes off the back of them. Jessie in her pink and green gear. Jock jumping on them. Braden in his dark blue jacket with a matching beanie on his head. His mind went back to the paints, the gift Braden had given him that no one else would have. How he came to them any time they needed him. Seeing him with Jessie. The feel of his hands on Wes.

He didn't want it to stop. None of it. He wanted more, and it was scary as fuck because he knew how temporary things were. Nothing in his life had ever really stuck, but he wanted Braden to.

Wes wasn't stupid. He knew he had been partially to blame, maybe more so with Alexander. He struggled opening himself up.

He didn't give himself to Alexander the way he should have...but Alexander hadn't been willing to fight for him, either. He'd easily been able to walk away. Christ, he hoped Braden wouldn't walk away. That he wouldn't disappoint the man.

Wes started going up the hill toward Braden and Jessie. They weren't too far ahead of him, Braden dragging because of the weight he carried. As though he knew Wes made his way toward them, he stopped and turned. His face was red because of the cold, but he smiled that happy fucking smile that only Braden gave, and he realized he would risk anything for it. For the first time, he would really risk anything.

"About time, Wesley," he said to Wes when he reached them. It was as though he knew what Wes had been thinking—as though he meant more than just Wes climbing up the hill.

"I'm here now."

"That's all that matters." He handed Jessie to him as the little girl wrapped her arms around his neck.

"Thank you," Wes told him but Braden just shook his head.

"You don't have anything to thank me for."

But he really did. "Come on. Let's get to the top."

The three of them, plus Jock, finished climbing up the hill. When they got to the top, Braden sat on the sled with Jessie between his legs and his arms around her. Then he scooted forward with them. "Get on here."

This is where Wes would usually second guess himself, but hell, he wanted to be like Braden—no hesitation at all. So he did. He climbed on behind Braden. They pushed off, Jessie cheering as they raced down the hill. Jock ran beside them, kicking up snow as they went.

They did it three more times, and on the fourth, when they made it to the bottom of the hill, the sled hit something and they all rolled off. Braden held Jessie again, Wes having held her the time before.

As soon as he hit the ground, he jerked into a sitting position, his heart hammering. "Jess, you okay?"

She lay on top of Braden and started laughing. "Hey. Not funny, Squirt." But he was laughing too. Then Wes fell onto his back, looking up at the sky, joining them.

"Let's do it again!" Jessie squealed.

"No," he and Braden both said at the same time, and he wondered, wondered if Chelle saw them right now, and hoped she thought they were doing a good job with Jessie. If he was doing a good job with himself.

Chapter Twenty-Six

They'd just finished Christmas dinner when Wes grabbed Braden's arm as he walked down the hall toward the bathroom.

"You're limping. What happened?" Wes asked him.

"Nothing. Fucked up my ankle a little that last time down the hill. It's no biggie."

Wes cocked his head a little, opened his mouth as though he was going to say something, but then kissed him instead. It took Braden a second to open his mouth, to let his tongue wrestle with Wes's, because he hadn't expected it. They were alone in the hallway, but still, Wes didn't usually do shit like this. He definitely didn't kiss Braden when anyone could walk by and see them. That made things more serious than Wes wanted them.

"What was that for?"

"I wanted to kiss you. Got a problem with it?" Wes teased.

"You got jokes now, Wesley, or what? Who are you, and what did you do with the Wes I know?" But he liked it. Fuck yeah, he liked it.

"You should have said something. I feel bad."

Braden brushed it off. "What would you have done? It's not a big deal. Hurts a little. It'll be fine by tomorrow."

"Aw, you don't like that you got hurt, do you? You're human, too. I know you can do just about anything, but looks like you're simply a man like the rest of us." Wes had laughter in his voice. He moved to walk down the hall and back to the living room, but this time it was Braden who grabbed his arm.

"Say it again."

"What?" Wes asked.

"The part where you said I can do anything."

Wes looked up and shook his head as if he didn't know what to do with Braden. "Only you."

"But you like me, remember?"

"I remember," Wes told him, and then walked away.

The rest of the night was pretty laid back. The kids ran around the house and played with their new toys. Braden and his dad took Wes to the shop to show him the motorcycle. Wes and Jessie called home and spoke with Lydia and her family. It was comfortable. They fit in with his family naturally, and Braden wondered if Wes realized it.

Since they'd had such a busy day, everyone when to bed early, including Wes and Jessie. Braden lay on the futon, staring into the dark, unable to sleep. His mom was right. He was in love with Wes. There was a small part of him that was a little freaked out over the idea just because—well, love was serious shit. It changed everything, especially with Jessie in the picture. Jock had always been the biggest responsibility he had—excluding his job. There was this little tug of fear that he hadn't expected—what if he fucked it up?

Braden shook his head, not willing to let himself think that way. He reached over and grabbed his phone.

U awake? He texted Wes.

Yeah. What if I wasn't, though?

U'd be awake now

Haha.

His fingers hovered over the screen, trying to figure out what else to say, or why he'd texted in the first place.

Jess ok?

He hoped like hell she wasn't having a night like she had Christmas Eve.

It took Wes a minute to reply.

Yes.

Ah, so it's just u who missed me.

What? You texted me.

Exactly.

There was another stall, but he didn't regret hinting that he missed him. Finally, Wes replied, and Braden hoped he wasn't pulling back again.

I'm glad I'm here.

Braden smiled into the dark.

Me too.

***

Today was their last full day with Braden's family. They had plans to go into Denver to an indoor mall with ice-skating, and other Christmas activities with the kids. Jessie was excited as hell to go. Wes could see Braden favor his ankle each time he stepped, and knew he was ignoring it for Jess.

"Hey. Maybe we should sit this one out," he told Braden as everyone was getting packed up to go. Like Wes knew he would, Braden shook his head.

"Nah. It's cool. She'll be heartbroken if we can't go. I'm fine. I'll just ice it and put it up tonight."

It was little things like that that showed Wes more and more than he wanted this man in his life. Wanted to keep him there. He took a step closer. "Braden—"

"Do you want us to take Jessie?" Emmy approached them. "Sorry, didn't mean to eavesdrop. Okay maybe just a little. But I wouldn't mind, if you think she'll be okay with it."

His immediate response was, "No, that's okay. Thanks, though." He didn't feel right with Jessie going with them if he and Braden weren't there. The only time she hadn't been with him since Chelle died was when she was in school, with Lydia, or Braden. Thinking of her in Denver without them made his stomach sour.

"Are you sure?" Emmy asked. "I know Brady won't stay unless someone forces him. Plus, we'd love to have her."

"Grandma and Papa spoil all the kids." Braden's sister Yvonne smiled as she walked by, her hand on her pregnant belly. Her words almost knocked him on his ass. Jessie wasn't their granddaughter. The poor kid didn't even know what it was like to have grandparents. He suddenly wished she did.

Emmy reached up and touched his cheek. "We'll take care of your girl, Wes."

The funny thing was, he didn't doubt it. Still, he wasn't sure…

Wes met Braden's eyes. "It's your call. You want to go, we'll go. If you think she'll be okay without us, we'll stay, and I'll make you take care of me." Braden winked.

"Shh. None of that in front of your mama. You let me know what you want to do, okay?" Emmy walked away.

"I'll be good if you wanna go." Braden leaned against the wall.

And he did…but he wanted to stay with Braden, too—to be here for him the way Braden was there for them. Yeah it was a silly, a sprained ankle, but walking around all day wouldn't help it. Skating would definitely be a no-go for him.

"Let me see how Jessie feels about it."

Braden nodded and Wes went into the living room, where Jessie was running circles with…he couldn't remember the little boy's name.

"Jess, come here for a second. I want to ask you something."

She made a beeline for him and wrapped her arms around his legs. Wes laughed before untangling her and kneeling down. "I'm not sure it's a good idea for Braden to walk around today because of his ankle. How would you feel if Emmy looked after you today and I stayed here to help Braden?"

She tried to roll her eyes but really just moved her whole head. "Silly, Uncle Wes. I'm a big girl, 'member? I want to go now. Can you ask Emmy if we can go now? I like her."

Well…that was easy. "Are you sure?"

She gave him another eye roll. Wes kissed her on the forehead. "Let me help you get into your jacket and everything. You guys are leaving in a minute."

She followed him to the hall closest where their coats were.

Braden happened to be standing there, too.

"You guys don't get to have any fun today." Jessie tugged on his shirt.

"I'm sure we'll figure something out. Will you drink a cup of hot chocolate for me?" Braden asked her. Jessie nodded her head. Fifteen minutes later, the clan of Roths plus Jessie filed out the door and climbed into a couple different vehicles. Through the front window he watched while Emmy fastened Jessie into a booster seat, and then they were gone.

"Wanted to be alone with me, huh?" Braden nudged him.

"Someone has to keep you out of trouble."

"Funny man. What do you want to do?"

"Food?" Wes asked.

"Food," Braden confirmed. They hadn't eaten this morning because they planned to get food in Denver.

They ate leftover ham from Christmas and some eggs at the kitchen table.

"Jess hasn't had any more problems since Christmas eve?" Braden asked him before eating a bite of ham.

Wes shook his head. "No. That was killer, though. It rips my heart out to see her like that."

"She's going to have her bad days and her good days. She's a happy little girl. You're incredible with her. You give her everything you can."

Those words penetrated any remaining armor Wes had. They meant the world to him. Not just because he loved Jessie so much, but because he was pretty sure he loved Braden, too. "Thanks, man. I…seriously, thanks. You are, too, though. She loves you."

Braden set his fork down, his eyes searching for something inside Wes. What, he didn't know, but he hoped Braden found it. "Guess you're gonna have to keep me around then."

"Guess so."

They finished eating, talking about nothing important. Afterward, they rinsed their dishes and then Wes said, "I need to go get cleaned up."

"You didn't already do that?"

"I had a kid to get ready, remember?" Wes laughed.

Braden followed him to his room, which was really Braden's room, and lay on the bed with his hands behind his head.

"Comfortable?" Wes asked as he stripped out of his clothes in the attached bathroom.

"Enjoying the view. I'd get in with you, but I'm not sure I can have sex in the shower with my ankle all screwed up."

Like he so often did around Braden, Wes smiled as he turned on the water and jumped in. "Who said I'd want to have sex with you in the shower?"

"Me. I even wanted to have sex with myself when I took one this morning. I'm irresistible like that."

Wes let out a loud laugh, pulled back the shower curtain, and said, "I've never known anyone like you."

"That a good thing, Wesley?"

No hesitation, Wes replied, "It is."

Chapter Twenty-Seven

Braden hated to sound cocky but he knew he was a good-looking man, knew he was likable. He never suffered in the date department, was used to getting compliments but hearing them from Wes made him feel invincible. Like he'd never really believed those things were true about himself but now could, because Wes said them. Maybe a little cheesy, but true.

Wes got out of the shower, dried off, then wrapped a towel around his waist.

"Hey. I was looking at your ass. What'd you cover it up for?" Goddamn, the man had a fine ass—firm, round globes that Braden wanted to grab on to.

Wes didn't reply to him, just playfully shook his head as he started brushing his teeth. Well, if he wouldn't respond, then Braden would just have to annoy the hell out of him until he did.

Pushing off the bed, he limped over and squeezed behind Wes. He slid his arms under Wes's, hugging him from behind, his fists clutching Wes's shoulders. "You smell good." He inhaled deeply.

"I'm brushing my teeth," Wes replied around his toothbrush.

"I can see that."

He didn't let go as Wes continued to brush, but then pulled back when he spit and then rinsed out his mouth and the toothbrush. As he went to put it back into the cup, Braden reached over and grabbed it, nudged Wes out of the way with his hip, and then put more toothpaste on.

"That's my toothbrush."

"Another thing I know." He winked before he popped it into his mouth and proceeded to brush his teeth.

Wes didn't stop him. Braden rinsed his mouth, too, put the toothbrush away, and their eyes met in the mirror. It was Wes who stood behind him now. Wes who pressed his lips to the back of Braden's neck, then his shoulder, let his teeth tease the muscle where the two met.

"I want you," Wes said against his skin. It made Braden's body burn, blood rush to his cock.

"What do you want to do to me?" He leaned back into his lover, who kept kissing.

"I want to fuck you."

"Not sure I heard you, Wesley. You're going to have to say it again."

"I." He bit into Braden's other shoulder. "Want. To." His hand roamed down the front of Braden's body, settling over his erection. "Fuck. You."

That's what he wanted to hear. He reached back and pulled Wes's towel free. "Only if you suck me off first."

Wes pushed him forward so Braden bent over the counter. "Not really sure you're in the position to make demands, B."

Ropes of desire tied him up, kept him from speaking for the first time in his life. He let out a moan when Wes kneeled behind him, wrapped his arms around Braden and unbuttoned and unzipped his jeans, before pulling them down. He ran his hands up and down Braden's thighs, callouses making it the rough kind of touch that drove him wild.

"Turn around." Wes licked the crease of his ass and he almost fucking came right then.

"You don't have to ask me twice." Braden turned, and as soon as he did, Wes's mouth was on him, enveloping him, before it was gone again.

Wes licked the crease between his crotch and his leg, let his tongue swirl around Braden's sac before he ran it from base to tip of his shaft.

"I want inside your mouth, Wesley. Take me deep." His voice was raspy, sex-filled, and he wondered if that got Wes harder.

And he listened to Braden, too, taking him as deep as he could. Braden knotted his hands in Wes's hair, guiding Wes as he blew him. Wes let him lead the way, let him rock into his mouth as Braden set the pace. He was fucking beautiful down there. The muscles in his neck and back contracted and flexed. His jaw stretched, and when he looked up at Braden, his eyes burned with lust. Braden knew Wes loved it as much as he did.

Braden let his hand drift from Wes's hair, cupped his cheek and brushed his thumb over his facial hair. Wes didn't slow his pace, kept sucking him off, kept holding his stare.

He's giving himself to me, Braden realized. Trying to tell Braden that he was his. There was nothing except Wes in his stare—no fear, no trepidation, no distance; probably for the first time ever. "You are so fucking incredible, Wesley. You are so fucking *mine*."

With that, Wes worked him faster, rolled Braden's balls in his hand as he swallowed around his dick.

"I'm going to come. Fuck, pull off, so I can come when you're fucking me."

Wes pulled back enough to say, "I want it. I'll get you hard again." And then he was back at it, sucking Braden like his life depended on it. If this killed anyone, though, Braden knew it'd be himself. But how the hell could he turn that down?

When the ache in his balls became too much, he didn't fight it back. Let the burn and goddamned euphoria take him over as he shot his load down Wes's throat. Wes swallowed it, then kept sucking, took the second jet that hit his tongue, too.

Braden's body felt like someone had taken all the bones out. It didn't stop him from pulling Wes to his feet, slipping his tongue into Wes's mouth because he suddenly really fucking needed to taste him. To own him. To taste himself on Wes and know he was a part of him.

When the kiss ended, he wrapped his arms around Wes's waist, letting the counter and Wes hold him up. "I don't know if I can ever orgasm again. You might have just rung me dry."

Wes chuckled. "I don't underestimate your abilities. Don't underestimate mine. I told you I'd get your hard again, and I will."

Braden had a feeling he'd enjoy the hell out of it, too.

He took off his shirt on the way to the bed. They spent what felt like an eternity kissing, stroking, licking, eating, playing…until he knew Wes had to be dying to come. His cock pulsed hard again.

"Told you I could get you up again," Wes told him with a smile. It hit Braden in the chest. Yeah, he so totally loved this man.

"I didn't doubt it for a second."

***

Wes grabbed lube and a condom from his bag. He was scared that all he'd have to do is touch his cock and the thing would erupt. That fear became even more real when Braden ripped the condom out of his hand, opened it, and then rolled it down Wes's shaft.

"You want me to fuck you, right?" he asked.

"Yeah."

"Then we better limit the touching."

Braden laughed, and pulled the lube out of Wes's hand next. He squirted some into his own hand, then tossed it to Wes.

Reaching between his legs, he lubed his asshole. Fuck, fuck, *fuck.* He really wanted to kill Wes.

"You want to do this or what?" He nodded at the bottle in Wes's hand.

Yeah. Okay. He could do this. Squirt lube into his hand, rub it on his dick. But all he could think about was Braden. The fact that Braden somehow filled him up even though it was Wes who was about to fuck him. That he felt him everywhere, in everything he did, and he wanted to celebrate that fact and tell Braden it freaked him out, too.

"I want it," was all he could say.

"How do you want me?"

Every. Way.

But instead of saying that, Wes laid on his back. Pulled Braden on top of him, his back on Wes's chest. He fisted his dick, found Braden's hole, then pushed inside.

The second he felt that tight, hot channel around him, his erection jerked. "Hold still a second. Fuck, you feel so good,

Braden."

When he got his body under control, Wes roped his arms around Braden, grabbing onto his shoulders. As he thrust up, he pushed Braden's body down. Each time they moved together, pleasure rocked through him, vibrated as if coming straight from Braden and into him. He kissed the back of Braden's neck as they fucked—thrusting up each time he pushed Braden down. He licked the tattoo on Braden's upper back, wanting to taste his skin.

His orgasm was right there, begging to explode but it somehow wasn't enough too. *Every way,* he'd thought, and that had been the truth. He wanted more.

Wes rolled them, still keeping their bodies connected as Braden now lay on his stomach on the bed, Wes flat on his back. He pulled out as far as he could before slamming forward again.

The curve of Braden's ass fit against his crotch. His hole hugged him tight as he made love to him.

"Fuck…right there. Harder, Wesley," Braden urged, and Wes obeyed. He pulled out to the tip again before pumping, thrusting, into Braden over and over.

More, more, more. Why the fuck couldn't he get enough?

Wes pulled out. "Turn over."

Braden did, lying on his back, facing Wes with his legs open for him. His dick looked painfully hard, gorgeous, swollen and veined as it rested against his stomach.

He jerked his eyes away, met Braden's, who said, "You're looking at me like you've never seen me before."

Maybe he hadn't. Or maybe he'd never seen himself. Wes wasn't sure, he just knew he needed more. He pushed inside Braden again. Braden, who wrapped his arms around him and squeezed his ass.

Wes thrust…fucked…made love to Braden. Braden kept one hand on Wes's ass, but with the other he jacked himself off. Wes's balls felt full, ached like they could pop. He leaned forward, pushed his tongue into Braden's mouth, and wondered if the man tasted himself there.

"Fuck. I'm gonna…"

He didn't get all the words out before he felt Braden stiffen, before ropes of white shot from his dick and into the space between them. That was all it took for Wes to follow, for pulse after pulse of cream to rip from him.

Like Braden said earlier, he felt like he might never come again as he collapsed on top of his lover.

Braden ran his hand up and down Wes's back as they both breathed heavily.

"Who else left you, Wesley?" Braden asked. "I know your dad left and your mom and Chelle died. Who else left you?"

His stomach felt like someone had set a bomb off inside it, but…but it didn't keep him from answering, because he wanted to give Braden everything he could.

"My boyfriend. Alexander." He'd known everything and yet he'd still just up and left Wes because Wes wasn't giving him what he wanted. Wes hadn't been enough to keep him.

"You were in love with him?"

"Yes."

"I hate him," Braden said with a mock chuckle. Wes appreciated the effort.

"We were together a long time. You know how I am, know that I'm distant. I was like that before I met him but I fell for him, anyway. We were together almost five years."

Braden kept stroking his back, and Wes found he needed it.

"I loved him but it wasn't enough. I came home from work one day and he had his shit packed. It wasn't that he'd met anyone else, he just…didn't love me anymore. He said he'd fallen out of love with me a long time before and couldn't keep pretending. Then he was gone."

"Hey." Braden tilted Wes's head up, with a finger under his chin, forcing Wes to look at him. "That's not me. I don't walk away. I won't leave you."

The bomb in his gut was suddenly gone. He'd handled losing Alexander. He'd really loved him, but he was over him now. Braden? He didn't ever want to have to get over losing him. He wasn't sure he could.

Wes leaned forward and kissed Braden deeply, slowly. Braden's hands cupped the sides of his head and made love to his mouth.

"Mmm, you can kiss, Wesley. Can I tell you something else?"

Before Braden could get the words out, his cell beeped. Wes rolled off him as Braden went to the bathroom and grabbed it from his pants. He hadn't needed to tell Braden they had to check it in case his mom called about Jessie. He'd somehow just known.

"My sister isn't feeling well so they're coming back early. We have about twenty minutes. Guess she knew we might need the heads up."

Well, there went that. Braden jumped in a quick shower while Wes cleaned up himself then the bed. The whole time he wondered what Braden had been about to tell him.

Chapter Twenty-Eight

Braden's sister relaxed most of the day. She wasn't really having contractions, she said, but she just didn't feel right, whatever that meant. The family spent the day around the house, laughing and talking.

Did Wes realize how well he fit with them? he wondered as he looked over and saw Wes sitting with his brother Evan, talking at the table. And Jessie obviously blended right in with the kids and the rest of his family. He hadn't expected anything less, but still it was good to see.

Especially since he'd almost told the man he loved him today. Braden would have been the first one to give a guy shit for saying he loved someone after sex, but things were different now. Wes made them different though he probably didn't even know it.

They all watched *A Christmas Story* after dinner and then they put the kids to bed. Jessie went easily, the trip having worn her out.

Braden went into the kitchen and grabbed himself and Wes a beer before going into the living room where his family all sat. Wes was in a chair, and Braden walked over to him, handed him a beer, and then sat on the floor between his legs.

"I still can't believe you don't know what you're having," he said to his sister Yvonne, who lay on the loveseat.

"You didn't want to know?" Wes asked her.

"We found out before but decided we wanted it to be a surprise this time," she told him.

"Not me. I couldn't handle that. I'm thinking it's a boy, though. You said you were naming him, Braden, right?" he teased Yvonne, who threw a pillow at him.

"I'm thinking one Braden is enough in this family."

"You can say that again!" Evan added.

"Hey. What'd I do?" Braden hung one of his arms over Wes's leg, surprised when the man laid a hand on his shoulder.

"You almost gave me a heart attack, more than all your brother or sisters combined," his mom said. "We never knew what you were going to do or say."

"And that's a bad thing?" he asked.

"I didn't say that." His mom looked at Wes, then back at Braden. "You may have always been surprising us, but we were always proud of you, too. You've never been one to back down to anything. You've always been a strong, honorable man."

Wes squeezed his shoulder and Braden looked up and winked at him.

"I took him to a basketball game when he was…oh, I don't know, about eight," his dad said.

"No, nine," Mom confirmed.

"Close enough." He rolled his eyes at her with a smile. "So we're at this game and the cheerleaders come out. Braden says, 'Wow dad, they're pretty.'"

Braden dropped his head back on Wes's lap, unable to believe they were going there.

His dad continued. "I told him yes and agreed. A minute later the team comes out, and this time Braden looks at me, dead in the eyes at nine years old, and says, 'Number twenty-one…he's cute, too.'"

Wes's hold on his shoulder loosened and Braden held his hand up, latching their fingers together. "Wow. They're trying to impress you for me. They're giving you my coming-out story," he teased, and Wes's grip tightened again.

"What did you do?" Wes asked his dad.

"Well, I about swallowed my tongue first. I wasn't sure what to say, but as I looked at him, I saw it, saw that he was testing me in a way. He was being honest, but he wanted to know it was okay, wanted to make sure I was okay. I'm not going to lie and say I wasn't confused, but he's my son, so I wasn't going to let him down, either. I told him yeah, that I could see how someone could think that. I told him it was okay for *him* to think that."

"Then he tells his dad, 'I know.' Can you believe that?" his mom added, and everyone in the room laughed.

"Then he grew up and dated every girl in our high school, including all my friends." Lizzy raised a brow at him.

"Hey… Not *all* your friends."

She rolled her eyes but it was Wes who spoke. "All women?"

Braden looked up at him again and nodded. "It wasn't as if we had a bunch of guys who were out at my high school."

"It had been so long since that basketball game and he'd never mentioned anything again." His mom set her hand on his dad's leg. "It didn't matter to us either way, but we just assumed the comment had been, I don't know, confusion, maybe? As I'm sure you know, Braden had more surprises for us, though."

Wes laughed, still holding his hand. "Why am I not surprised about that? What he do then?"

"He came home one day his senior year in a horrible mood. He's so easygoing we almost never see him mad, but that day—"

"I was pissed." He had been.

His mom picked up the story again. "I asked him what happened, and he said there was a boy at his school who they found out was gay—Gavin, great boy. I'd never heard of him at the time, though. He wasn't someone that Braden spent time with."

"He was in the band," Braden told Wes.

"He was a shy kid, but so sweet. Everyone was giving him a hard time when they found out, though, Braden's friends included, teasing him and such. So I asked Braden what he did, and he looked me in the eye, shrugged and said, 'Asked him to prom.' I won't say I wasn't worried. His father and I told him that, too. There are a bunch of—excuse my language, but…ignorant assholes out there. I was worried that he didn't know what he was doing, or that he'd done that just for Gavin. But he told me, sat me down and told me, 'I like boys, too, Ma.

"That was all we needed to know. Sure we were still worried, but we were proud as hell of him at the same time. The school fought him, but he took that boy to prom. I don't know how he realized it, but he knew that if he accepted Gavin, others would, too. Gavin never hung out with Braden when he was with his friends—too different—but they accepted him because Braden did. They accepted Braden with a boyfriend, and they never gave Gavin trouble after that. Bless his heart. It wasn't as if that poor boy didn't have enough to deal with."

Braden tugged Wes's hand and Wes leaned over him. "See? You landed yourself a pretty incredible man." He winked and Wes smiled. He'd never get enough of that smile.

***

"A conceited man." Wes shook his head but kissed Braden on the forehead before sitting up again.

"I didn't know Braden had a boyfriend in high school." He looked at Braden's family, fully knowing where Braden got his traits from. They were good people, good people who loved their family unconditionally. He was honored to be there with them.

"High school and after. The dummy moved halfway across the

United States with him after graduation," Bill grumbled.

Whoa. He didn't know that. Not that it mattered, but he didn't expect it.

"Oh, Bill. Stop it." Emmy smacked his leg. "Gavin is a good man, and it wasn't halfway across the United States."

"I never said he wasn't, I just always knew he wasn't the one for Braden. Don't pretend you didn't, either."

"Okay, I'm thinking that's about enough of the Family Braden Hour. I went, I had fun. It wasn't just for Gavin. You knew I never wanted to stay around here after school, Dad. That just wasn't my thing. I always planned on exploring."

"Here we go again," Lizzy groaned.

So this was obviously a conversation they'd had before, and as much as Wes probably should agree with Braden and want them to stop, curiosity nagged at him.

"You have to admit, the way you did it wasn't the best way, Brady. You came to us after graduation and said you were leaving in a couple days. I get it. I understand what Gavin was going through, and I know you. That's what you do. When someone needs you, you're there. You jump right in and do whatever they need, even if it's not what's best for you. You've always been the first to make sacrifices like that, because you have this strong sense of honor. But you know it hurt us, too. And you know deep down you made yourself think you cared about Gavin more than you did, because he always felt like he needed you."

With each word that Emmy spoke, Wes's gut sank deeper.

Braden's vow from earlier slammed into Wes. *That's not me. I don't walk away. I won't leave you.*

Was he with Wes because he wanted to be, or because that's just who Braden was? From the beginning, he'd been the first one try and help Wes out—because of what? The sense of honor that his parents spoke of? Because from the way they made it sound, that's the way he'd been with Gavin, too.

"There's more to the story than you guys know, and that's all I'm going to say about it." There was finality in Braden's voice that Wes had never heard from him before.

The family went on talking about other things, but Wes's mind was still on what he'd heard. He head a heaviness in his chest that he'd thought long gone since things with he and Braden had gotten more serious.

Alexander had fallen out of love with him, yet stayed out of responsibility before just walking out one day, the same way his father had walked out on his mom. Not that Braden was in love with him—those words had never left his mouth—yet he'd stayed, stuck around, brought Wes and Jessie here because they'd needed him. What happened when Braden realized that wasn't enough? When he didn't want to be stuck in the kind of town he never permanently wanted to be in, or didn't want the responsibilities that came with Wes? When he did what was best for him rather than what he thought was best for Wes and Jessie? Braden did a lot of thoughtful things, but that's just who he was. He said he loved Jessie, and Wes didn't doubt that. Still, he loved his family, yet picked up and left them. Is that where Jessie and he stood, too?

He hadn't realized he squeezed Braden's hand tighter until the man looked up at him, questions in his eyes. Wes shook his head as if to say he was okay, but he really didn't know if he was. It made him nauseous to think of Braden being with them—of sticking around because that's just what he did. That it was just who he was. He didn't walk away when he committed to doing something. He needed Braden with him because it's where he wanted to be.

Wes tried to keep his head in the game the rest of the night, but his mind stayed in the conversation Braden's family had had.

Braden must have realized it, because when they were all saying their goodnights, he stopped Wes in the hallway.

"Hey, everything good?" he asked. Wes looked down,

distracted by Jock, who sat at Braden's feet.

"You never told me how he got his name?" he asked.

Braden's brows pulled together but he answered, "I named him Tom when I first got him, but soon realized the dog had a crazy obsession with jockstraps. He got a name change pretty quickly."

"Tom?" It wasn't as if any of this mattered, and he wasn't even sure why he'd brought it up.

"From *Tom and Jerry*, of course. What's up with you, Wesley?" Braden stepped forward, boxing Wes between his body and the wall.

"Nothing." He shook his head. "I just have a lot on my mind. I'm gonna hit the sack. I know we're leaving early in the morning."

Braden frowned but still stepped back so Wes could move. When Wes got to his bedroom door, Braden's words stopped him. "Hey. I'm not going anywhere. Whatever you need, I'm here."

He couldn't help but wonder if he'd said something similar to Gavin.

Chapter Twenty-Nine

"Mom says you're welcome back anytime. Lydia and the kids can come too, ya know." Braden looked over at Wes as they drove back home. He'd been quiet since last night, though Braden wasn't sure why. He was about ready for it to end, though.

"Your family is great. That's nice of them."

Which wasn't a, *sure, I'd love to go!* Or even a, *we'll see.*

Braden glanced into the backseat at Jessie, who was coloring. He had to bite his tongue not to ask Wes what the fuck was going on, but he knew it wasn't right to do it in front of her.

The rest of the ride was just like the first part, sporadic conversation here and there, always started by Braden and Wes being hardly involved.

By the time they pulled into the driveway, Jessie was passed out in the cab, with Jock's head in her lap.

"I'll grab the stuff if you want to carry her in," Braden said softly as not to wake her.

Wes nodded. A few minutes later, Braden leaned against the back of Wes's couch as the man carried Jessie to her bedroom. Jock jumped on the couch and laid down as if he belonged here.

"She stay asleep?" Braden asked when Wes came back into the living room.

"Yeah. She had a big few days. I'm sure she's exhausted."

Braden was, too, but instead of getting ready to go home, he asked, "You want to have a drink or something? Or if you want, we can work on Chelle's room again."

Wes's eyes dulled with sadness. "No. I'm pretty tired. I was thinking about taking a nap, too."

That was a hint if Braden had ever heard one. Too bad for Wes he planned to ignore it. "Hey. Come here."

He thought for a minute Wes would refuse, but he ended up walking over to Braden. He wrapped his arms around Braden's waist and leaned his forehead against Braden's. Wes felt good there. He felt right.

"You sure everything's okay? You're being 'Grumpy Wes.' I thought we'd seen the end of him."

Wes didn't laugh like he'd hoped he would. "I just have a lot of shit on my mind."

"Hey, this isn't about Gavin, is it? You don't need to be jealous, Wesley. It wasn't serious with him. Hell, I've never really been serious with anyone—"

"Yet you left your family to move with him?" Wes cut him off too soon for him to add the "before." "Why would you do that for someone you weren't in love with?"

Braden shrugged. "Because it was the right thing to do. He wouldn't have gone without me and he needed to go. Is that really what this is about? Yeah, Gavin and I dated. We weren't serious but we dated, and he's a good friend of mine. It wasn't like…" *Like it is with us.* Why were the words still stuck in his mouth?

Wes pulled back. "That'd make me a pretty big asshole if I was jealous because of a past relationship. That's not…" He shook his head. "I'm just trying to figure shit out. You know how I get. I just…just let me figure it out."

Anger surged through him, squeezing in and filling all the space inside him. After spending five days with him, after Braden falling for him, he needed to figure shit out?

"Figure what out? You've been figuring things out since we met. Listen, I get it. I know you have Jessie to worry about, but I love that kid. You know I wouldn't hurt her. I feel like I'm running in circles with you."

Circles he thought had ended. Braden pushed around him, pacing the room. Didn't Wes get it?

"I didn't ask you to do that, Braden. You knew I had stuff going on. You're the one who pushed."

"Fuck you, Wes. Of course you didn't ask me to do anything, because that would mean you gave a shit about something. We all know you can't do that. God forbid you come out of that bubble you keep yourself locked in."

Wes flinched as though Braden punched him, making guilt slam into Braden. "Fuck. I didn't mean that. I—"

"Yeah, you did. If that's how you feel, why the fuck stay?" Wes raised his voice but seemed to realize it. After he eyed the hallway, his voice lowered, but no less filled with anger. "Because that's what you do, right? You stick around when you think someone needs the great Braden Roth. You make it better, whether you want to be there or not."

Braden's body buzzed with anger and fury. But buried beneath that rage was hurt. "I don't even know what the hell you're talking about. Christ, if you're scared, admit you're scared. Don't put this on me. I'm always here, *always*. I've changed my whole life since you and Jessie." He never went out anymore, didn't pick up extra shifts anymore. His idea of a good time was eating pizza and hanging out with them—and he wanted that. Wanted it more than he'd ever wanted anything. Wanted to feel settled the way only they made him.

Wes was silent. His chest rose and fell with heavy breaths, his eyes distant like they used to be. "Well, I'm sure you'll be happy to have your old life back now, then." His words sounded hollow; hollow and sad.

Just how Braden felt. "And I guess you'll just keep on running."

Braden called Jock, and then the two of them walked out the door. Wes didn't try to stop them.

***

Wes sat in Lydia's kitchen a few days later, waiting for her to ask what was going on. Jessie was playing video games with her cousins in the living room. Lydia paced back and forth through the room, glancing at him every so often but not speaking.

"If you have something to say, Lyd, please, just say it. I can't play games right now." Because the truth was, he fucking hurt. This whole thing left a gaping hole inside him that felt like it got bigger and bigger by the second. Like it would swallow him.

"Jessie said she had a wonderful time over Christmas."

"She did," he nodded. "We all did."

"Then what's going on now? If you think I can't tell something happened, you're crazy. Jessie asked me where Braden's been. What did you do?"

His eyes jerked toward hers. "Because I automatically did something?"

"If I'm being honest, yes."

Ouch. If that wasn't his cue to leave, he didn't know what was. Wes pushed to his feet. "I love you, Lyd, I do, but I can't do this with you right now."

"Don't do this, Wes. I don't want you to be alone. What are you punishing yourself for?"

He took a deep breath, but didn't turn back around to look at her. "I'm not punishing myself. I'm tired of losing everyone I love,

Lyd. I am. I just…" *Need him to want to be with me.* He couldn't handle Braden being with him just because he's the kind of guy who doesn't walk away.

"Just what?" she asked.

"I'm tired. I'm just tired. I'm going to grab Jess and head out. We'll see you soon."

She didn't say a word as he went into the living room and got Jessie ready to go home. "Do you want to grab some pizza?" he asked Jessie when they got to the car.

"Yay! Pizza!" She bounced in her booster seat so he took that for a yes. It didn't take long to get their food. They ate dinner together at the table and then settled onto the couch to watch TV.

"Uncle Wes?" she asked before he had a chance to turn the television on.

"Yeah, kiddo?"

"Where's Uncle Braden?" Every muscle in his body cramped up at the question. It had been less than a week since they'd come, home but she was so used to seeing him, she missed Braden already.

"Well, I think he might be at work today. I know he misses

you, though. Even when he can't see you, he misses you." He didn't want her to ever think this had anything to do with her. If there was one thing Wes couldn't deny, it was the fact that Braden did love Jessie.

"I like playing with him. He's good at coloring."

"And playing in the snow," Wes added.

"And bowling."

He tickled her sides. "And giving you too many sweets." She laughed and Wes did too.

When she stopped giggling, she spoke again. "He's good at lots of things, just like you."

Wes's heart ached a little at that. Was he? Was Wes good at a lot of those same things Braden was? Did he make her laugh and…hell, was he a nice person the same way Braden was?

"Is he gone like Mommy?" she asked, wiping her eyes. Wes's chest cracked apart. His whole body did.

"No, baby girl. He's not. Braden is okay. There's just a lot going on." It was a strange moment to realize it, but Wes noticed she never said "says" anymore when speaking about her mom. It was always "said." It made his throat feel tight. It meant she really started to grasp that Chelle was gone.

"Is he not your boyfriend anymore?" she asked, breaking his heart. He didn't realize she really got what was going on between them.

"It's hard to explain, kiddo. Hey, what do you say we go look at puppies tomorrow?"

Jessie shook her head. "I want Jock."

Wes sighed, not sure what to say.

"I miss Braden." She dropped her head on his arm, and Wes wrapped it around her. "I hope we get to see him soon."

Wes sighed. "I miss him, too, kiddo." He missed him, too.

Wes clicked power on the TV and turned it to *Tom and Jerry* and watched it with her. A couple hours later, Jess was fast asleep, and Wes stood in front of Chelle's closed door. He'd started this with Braden, started trying to move on, to move forward, yet hadn't been back since the only day they'd spent in the room.

Chelle would hate him for keeping his emotions on lockdown. She always hated the fact that Wes thought things were easier when he was alone. He hadn't felt alone when he'd sat in that room with Braden. And if he didn't do this, didn't say goodbye to his big sister, he might never be able to move forward. The only way to move forward was to deal with the past.

It was time Wes finished in here. He needed to be strong enough to do it on his own. He needed to be strong for Jessie, and for himself.

Chapter Thirty

Braden stood in the kitchen of the firehouse when Fred and a couple of the other guys came in. There was a group of three of them, talking as they went and not paying much attention to what they were doing.

As they passed him, Fred's arm bumped into Braden's. He looked up as though to apologize to who he hit, until he saw it was Braden and just turned to keep going.

Without any thought, Braden's arm shot out and he grabbed Fred. "You hit me."

"So?"

He felt like his insides were on fire, burning with anger.

"Why's it so hard for you to know I have a boyfriend?" Braden took a step closer to him. "Always wanted one but didn't have the balls to go for it? Let me tell you, you're really missing out." He winked at Fred, and that's when the man went for him.

He swung at Braden, who tried to dodge it. Fred's fist grazed his cheek enough that he felt the sting of the hit.

Braden wouldn't miss. He let his fist fly, making contact with Fred's eye. Before he could have another go at him, arms wrapped around him from behind. Someone else grabbed onto Fred, who yelled. "You son-of-a-bitch! Don't you ever say shit like that to me again!"

Braden's chest hurt he breathed so hard. "You forgot to add queer in there, because that's what I am, remember? And I like it, too."

Fred tried to go after him again, yelling and cussing like crazy. Both of them went still when the chief walked into the room. "Braden, Fred. What the fuck's going on here?"

"Nothing," they both said at the same time. The hold on Braden loosened, and Fred pulled free of his and walked out of the kitchen.

"Roth, in my office," the chief said before heading that way. Braden groaned and followed him. He closed the door behind them and collapsed into the chair.

"Want some ice for that nothing on your face?" he asked.

"What nothing?" Braden leaned back.

"This isn't like you. What's going on?"

A deep breath escaped his lungs. He was right. Braden wasn't being himself at all. "Nothing."

The other man shrugged. "Listen, I know we haven't talked about this in a while, but I was talking with a buddy of mine in New York. He's got an opening coming up. I know you were looking to get out of here, and what better place than The Big Apple? I can put in a good word for you."

His stomach dropped out at the same time his pulse picked up, adrenaline rushing through him. New York. It was a dream of his, being in that city. He'd thought of going many times, and now was the perfect time, but...the weights in his gut got heavier.

"Is this because of that shit with me and Fred?"

The chief looked confused as he replied, "No, it's because you came to me months ago and asked me to keep an eye out for you with some of the people I know. I don't want to lose you, but I don't want you here if your heart's not in it. You came to me, not the other way around."

Yeah, but that had been before. Before Jessie. Before *Wes.* Wes, who he loved. Wes, who he didn't want to leave. Wes, who was done with him.

"Can I have a couple days to get back to you?" Braden asked him.

"Yeah. And it's not a guarantee, either. I can sing your praises, which I will, but it might not be enough. I have a good feeling about it, though."

Which meant he was close enough that his word would mean a lot.

Braden stood. "Thanks. I appreciate that."

The chief nodded. "You and Fred do need to figure this shit out, though. I'll talk to him, too but you know as well as I do we can't have discord in a place like this. You have lives in your hands."

Yeah, he knew it. The chief was right. "We'll work it out."

Braden walked out of the office, wanting to talk to Wes. Hoping the man would ask him to stay. If not, looked like he'd have a new adventure in the form of New York City.

***

Tuesday night, as Wes lay in bed, his phone rang. He thought about ignoring it, but rolled over and plucked it off his bedside table.

He felt like an idiot because his heart rate kicked up when he saw Braden's name light up the screen.

"Hey." Wes moved to his back.

"Hey."

Neither of them spoke for a few moments until Braden said, "Tomorrow's Wednesday. Can I pick Jessie up from school and stay with her?"

The word "no" wasn't even a consideration. No matter what went down with them, Wes wouldn't take Jessie away from seeing Braden as long as he wanted to. "Yeah, sure. She misses you."

"I miss her, too. We need to talk afterward, Wes. There's something I need to tell you."

For the first time in his life, he wished someone called him Wesley instead of Wes. "Okay."

"Cool. I'll let you go. You know, so I can get back to my old life and all." Before Wes could reply, Braden added, "Shit. I'm sorry. I'm being a prick."

"Eh. I've been known to be one before, too."

Braden chuckled. "Yeah, you have. Listen, I'm gonna go. I'll talk to you tomorrow."

Wes didn't sleep the rest of the night. When the alarm went off to get Jessie ready for school, he already sat on the edge of his bed…in Chelle's old room. When he told Jessie he planned to sleep in there, she didn't even bat an eye at him. That didn't mean she wouldn't have questions later, but for now she seemed fine.

He got them both ready, dropped Jessie off at Lydia's for her to take her to school in a little while, and then drove to work. They were the on-call trauma hospital tonight, which meant they were crazy busy.

They had patients from a four-car accident come in, and of course he had the ER. By the time he got home, all he wanted to do was have a beer and go to bed.

The second he walked into the house he realized there was something else he wanted to do. Fuck Braden, kiss him, hug him—at this point, he was willing to take anything. Braden stood with his hands shoved into his jean pockets, the firm shape of his muscles pressing against the fabric.

Braden cocked a brow at him, obviously knowing what he was thinking. Leave it to Braden not to hold that knowledge back, either.

They had dinner, and then Braden played with Jock while he bathed Jessie. After TV, and homework, which their teacher gave them to prepare for Kindergarten, he was about to put Jessie to bed when Braden called her over to him. "You be a good girl, okay?" He hugged her.

"I will, silly Braden."

"Love you, Squirt."

Wes watched the scene play out in front of him with a lump in his throat. There was something different about the way Braden spoke to her tonight. Something that made him hurt clear down to his bones.

He stalled putting Jessie to bed, dread swimming around inside him. When Wes went back into the living room, he saw the front door cracked open and knew Braden must be on the covered porch.

"You moved into the big room," was the first thing he said to Wes when Wes joined him outside.

"It was time."

"Good for you."

"I haven't gone through the chest at the foot of the bed. It was important to her. It doesn't feel right going through that stuff. She's had it since she was a kid."

"It's a start. You'll get there."

"What's going on, Braden?" Braden wasn't one to avoid a topic, and the fact that he did stressed Wes out.

"I got asked about a job in New York…trying to decide if I should take it or not."

No, fought to jump off Wes's tongue as the same time his whole body went numb. Braden had been saying goodbye. He'd just told Jessie goodbye. "New York?" His tongue felt swollen, like he had cotton mouth, the way he did when he used to get high as a teenager.

"Yep. Do I have a reason not to go, Wes?"

His first thought was, *now there's the Braden I know.* He comes right out and says whatever's on his mind. But he also didn't say he *didn't* want to go. And how could Wes ask him not to? It was just the kind of thing Braden would thrive at. He'd told Wes himself that he wanted to explore, that he never settled down in one place too long.

"It sounds like something you'd like to do," were the only words Wes could manage to push out. His throat squeezed so tight, he hardly got those out.

Braden watch him a second, and then stood. "I guess I have an answer, then." He took a step, stopped, then turned around. Reaching out, he cupped Wes's cheek, his hands rough, and, despite the weather, somehow warm. "You're too fucking sexy for your own good. You take care of yourself, Wesley. I'll be back to say goodbye to Jess before I go. Can I keep in touch with her?"

"You know the answer to that, man."

With that, Braden Roth walked away from him. It made Wes's chest ache in a way it never had, a million times worse than with Alexander. No matter how much his legs twitched to run and his throat opened up to speak, he just stood where he was. It fucking killed him, but Wes did the...right thing. He gave Braden the freedom he deserved. He let him go.

Chapter Thirty-One

Braden set the shot glass down on the bar with a loud clank. Manson…Mason…whatever his name was looked over at him with raised a brow. He picked up a towel and flung it over his shoulder, with his green eyes still on Braden.

"What?" Braden finally asked.

"Nothin'." Mason wiped down the counter and handed a beer to another customer. Since it was a weeknight, the band wasn't in. Music still filled the room, but without the heavy bass as it spilled from speakers hung on the walls.

Eh. Wasn't like he wanted to talk to the man, anyway.

Braden spun the glass around. Wasn't like he felt like getting shitfaced drunk, either. That wasn't really his style. But sitting at home just made him too antsy. It made his mind run on too many things he didn't want to think about.

"Want anything else?" Mason asked him.

"Coke?"

"Don't sell drugs here."

"Ha ha. Very funny."

Mason smirked and filled up a glass of soda for him. It took Braden nearly an hour to suck it down. By the time he did, the bar was empty, except for him and Mason.

"Braden, right?" the man asked.

"Yep."

"Wanna play a game?" He nodded toward the pool table.

Wasn't like Braden had anything better to do, so he stood, and said, "Sure."

Mason opened up the table and pulled the balls out.

"Perks of being the owner?" Braden chuckled.

"Yep." He used the same word Braden had a minute before.

Mason racked the balls and Braden broke. He made stripes. Damn it. He always played better with solids.

"Mopey isn't a good look on you," Mason said, mid-game.

"Didn't ask." He definitely wasn't in the mood for this. He didn't even know this guy. It wasn't like he wanted to talk to him about shit. "He doesn't want me to go. I know he doesn't. He's freaked out but I don't get why. I know he has issues, but we were getting past them." So much for not talking.

"Sexy guy with the sad eyes you were dancing with the other night?" Mason leaned against the table.

"His eyes aren't sad. Not all the time."

"Not when he's dancing with you, they aren't."

"Who are you again?" Braden aimed and took a shot.

"I'm the bartender. Everyone talks to the bartender, remember?" He laughed.

Braden couldn't muster one up. "Not me. Your shot."

Mason hit two balls in before he missed. "If you don't want to talk, get laid. That always helps."

He cleared the table before he spoke again. "I'm not looking to fuck."

What the hell was Wes's problem? Had Braden misread him? Did he not feel the same way about Braden that Braden felt about him?

Mason laughed. "You used to everyone wanting you, or what? You're sexy, too, but I wasn't offering. I don't fuck guys who are in love with someone else. It's messy, and I don't do messy."

Well that made him feel like an asshole. "You're right. I'm sorry. I just… I thought things were getting better. I don't understand how he can walk away."

"I thought we weren't doing this? You don't talk to bartenders, remember?"

He had to admit the man was funny, and if he wasn't in such a shitty mood, he'd laugh. "We're not."

They played for a few minutes. It was Mason who spoke again. "So what happened?"

"Hell if I know. He freaked out. I told him I got a job offer, and he told me to go."

Mason frowned. "Maybe it's the right thing. Doesn't sound like either of you fought much for each other."

"No offense, but you don't know shit. You don't know us." But a little voice inside his head knew Mason was right, but Braden felt like he fought for them their whole relationship. It was Wes who didn't love him enough to do the same.

***

Wes looked at the envelope sitting in the middle of the kitchen table. He picked it up, then put it back where he'd set it about an hour before.

It had his name on it.

In Chelle's handwriting.

Part of him wanted to shove it back into the chest. To put it away and not read it. But he knew he couldn't. The bigger part of him wanted to know what it said.

He collapsed into the chair, grabbed the envelope, and opened it.

Wes,

You know I'm sitting here wondering how long it took you to find this, right? I left it right on top of the trunk for easy access, but I also know it probably took you a while to open it. As soon as I thought about that, I started to get frustrated, but then I realized that's just always been you, ya know? Even when you were a kid, you didn't rush into anything. You've always guarded yourself, even before the bad things started to happen. You've always been cautious, making sure someone or something was worth your love or your time, before you devoted it. I'm not going to pretend there weren't times I wanted to knock sense into you, or if I were still alive that I probably wouldn't often want the same thing now, but do you know what I love about you? It may take you longer to put yourself out there, but when you do it, it's with 100% of who you are. You'd probably be arguing with me about that, but it's true, little brother. Maybe Alexander couldn't see it, maybe you can't see it, but I promise you, most of us do.

That's why I wanted you to have Jessie. I knew no one would love her like you. No one would always put her first the way you will. I can go easier knowing she has you to love her.

Do me a favor, though, okay? Try and be happy. Realize how great a guy you are and that you're worth love and happiness. It's worth it to put yourself out there, even if you do get hurt. If you don't risk your heart, you'll never know what it's like for it to fully be whole.

If you don't do it for yourself, do it for me. I'm holding you to that, which is shitty of me, but what are sisters for? ☺.

Love,

Chelle

Wes held the letter in his hands, the words blurred, swimming in the wetness of his eyes. He wanted to be the person Chelle thought he was. He wanted to be the best he could be for Jessie. He wanted to prove to himself that he was worth it—even if things didn't turn out the way he wanted. He wanted to be the guy who fought for the man he loved, and he sure as hell wasn't doing that now.

Wes pushed to his feet, hoping it wasn't too late.

Chapter Thirty-Two

Braden still couldn't get Mason's words out of his head. He just didn't know what to do about them. The man couldn't have been more right—he'd given up on Wes. But hell, how much could he keep pushing? How much could he try to be in Wes's life before he got the message? If Wes wanted them there, he knew Braden would be, and the fact was, he wasn't the type of guy to be in this alone, no matter how much Braden loved him.

He needed Wes to put himself out there for Braden, too.

Braden climbed into his truck after work, weariness taking root in his muscles.

He let his truck rumble to life and steered it toward his house, and Jock. It didn't take long to get there. His body felt more drained with each step he took.

Braden fumbled with his keys and pushed the door. He knew something was wrong when Jock didn't take him down when he stepped inside.

He let his eyes raise to the couch and—"Breaking and entering?"

Wes grinned at him from where he sat. "I figured you're worth the risk of Jock trying to eat me."

Braden laughed at that. Jock could never hurt a fly. "Glad you were willing to brave my killer dog for me." He tossed his keys to the coffee table. When he tried to walk by the couch and to the kitchen, Wes reached out and grabbed his wrist.

"You're worth more risk than that."

Braden's heart thundered, annoyance and hope colliding

inside him. "You didn't think so a few days or weeks ago." He pulled his arm free, but then sat down.

"Not going to make this easy on me, are you?"

"Nah, but neither of us would want it that way."

Even though Wes didn't reply, Braden knew he agreed with him.

"I freaked. I know that's not an excuse, but when I heard that story about Gavin..."

"I wasn't in love with him. We dated, and then we were good friends, but I was never in love with him."

"But you went with him. You left your family without much notice and uprooted your life because someone you didn't love needed you. Jesus, that's an incredible thing to do, Braden, but I didn't want that for us."

Braden shook his head. "What are you talking about?"

"Us. Me. We fucked the first night because I was lonely, and we got closer because I needed your help with Jess, with Chelle's room. It was always me needing you. I don't want you to make sacrifices because you're honorable."

Braden couldn't help it, he laughed at that. "All of this happened because you think I don't want to be with you?"

"Gavin—"

"Wasn't you. I'll admit shit with him started because—hell, I don't know. Because I thought I could make things better for him, or get people to accept him. Maybe I do have some sort of hero complex. But me leaving with him had nothing to do with us. He was my excuse, Wesley. If I went because of him, I didn't have to feel bad for leaving. We both had our reasons, his a whole lot more serious than mine, but I was young, and I wanted to see more of the world. Leaving with him just gave me a reason to go without feeling guilty. Gavin and I both knew that. It's just my parents who didn't."

He grabbed the back of Wes's neck and pulled him closer. "You dumb son of a bitch. I've never wanted to be with someone the way I want to be with you. And I guess this is partially my fault for never telling you, but fuck, I've never wanted someone the way I want you, Wesley. I push and push my way into any situation because I'm used to getting what I want, and…I didn't want it to be that way with you. I didn't want to screw it up by going too fast or…" He shook his head, knowledge planting there.

"I guess I needed to know you really wanted to be with me, too. I've never worried about shit like that before, but with you…hell, Wesley, everything's different with you."

***

Wes's whole body felt like it was overheating. He could hardly hear Braden over the bass in his ears, but somehow he still knew what the man was saying. "You're stealing my thunder, Braden."

Braden's eyebrows pulled together. Wes didn't answer his

silent question, just stood and nodded his head at Braden for the man to follow him. He led the way to Braden's room.

"You really took this breaking and entering thing seriously, didn't you? What were you doing while I was at work?" Braden teased as they stood at the bedroom door. Again, Wes didn't reply.

He opened the door to Braden's room and stood there, waiting. Nerves increased the bass, but he ignored it. Ignored everything as Braden stepped into the room. As he silently walked away from Wes.

"You wanted me to paint you a picture, so I did. I didn't have time to do anything more than that, but I figured that's the most real thing I can give you. Even if you say no, I'd understand it. I'd still want you. We'd find a way to make it work—"

"Shut up, Wesley." Braden stopped in front of the canvas resting on the wooden easel. "You're really askin' me this?"

"I am. Maybe it's wrong of me and I'm being selfish. I understand if you have to say no, but I needed to do it. I needed to risk my heart, because you're worth it. And I'm worth it, too."

Wes's legs tingled as though they'd fallen asleep. He walked toward Braden and looked down at the canvas with him, at the four red letters in the middle of it.

STAY

"Or we can go if you want us to. I'll talk to Jess—"

"I said shut up, Wesley." Braden turned to face him. "I've had family but I've never had real roots before you. I've never had someone or something that made me want to stay until you. I'm crazy, fucking in love with you, Wesley. I'd rather be here with you and Jessie than anywhere else in the world. I *fit* with you. I'm settled for the first time in my life with you. With both of you. It's more fun sitting around at night hanging out with you guys than any of the old shit I used to do."

Fuck, he wanted that, too. Wanted it more than he'd ever wanted anything else.

"I guess it's good that I'm crazy, fucking in love with you, too. I watched other people walk in and out of my life and never felt enough to fight for them. I've never loved them enough. I'd take on anything for you."

Wes stepped closer and pressed his mouth to Braden's.

"I told you that you liked me," Braden whispered. Wes smiled against Braden's lips as he kissed him again.

"Not like. *Love* you. You're crazy, and don't know when to keep your mouth shut, but I wouldn't have it any other way. Still, are you sure you want to stay? I know you—"

"I don't want to go. I never did. I just needed you to give me a reason to stay."

"You have one now," Wes told him.

Braden grinned and nodded at the painting. In one corner it has "For Braden," because Wes had used the canvas Braden made out to himself.

"You signed it 'Wesley,' not Wes."

"That's because I want to be someone different for you, different than I am with anyone else. I'm only Wesley with you."

Braden nodded, emotion in his eyes Wes had never seen. "You are. But you're still painting me another picture."

He laughed the way only Braden could make him. "I will. I'll paint you a thousand of them if it makes you stay."

"The only thing I need to make me want to stay is you....is our family. Come on. Let's go get Jess."

Wes had lost a lot in his life—parents, his sister, dreams—but what he often didn't do was take the time to look at the things he had. Lydia, who would do anything for him. Jessie, who he loved more than anyone in this world. And Braden, the man who stole his heart. The man he gladly gave it to. The man who chose him the way Wes would always choose Braden, no matter how hard it was. He had everything he needed, and he couldn't wait to start living—not just getting by, but *living* their life together.

The End

Return to Blackcreek in Mason's story, coming soon.

ACKOWLEDGEMENT:

Thanks to my editor, and beta readers. Also to Jamie for coming through like always. A huge thanks goes to my readers. Thanks for taking this journey with me. I hope you guys are enjoying the ride as much as I am. My family... I couldn't do this without your support. Thank you.

COLLIDE—Blackcreek, book one:

At ten years old, Noah Jameson and Cooper Bradshaw collided mid-air when they dove for the same football. For three years, they were inseparable...until one day when Noah and his parents disappeared in the middle of the night.

Noah and Cooper never knew what happened to each other. Now, seventeen years later, after finding his boyfriend in bed with another man, Noah returns to Blackcreek looking for a fresh start. And damned if he doesn't find his old friend grew up to be sexy as sin. Coop can't believe Noah—the only person he trusted with the guilt over his parents' death—is back. And gay... Or that Cooper himself suddenly wants another man in his bed for the first time.

There's no denying the attraction and emotion between them, but can they overcome the ghosts of their pasts to have a future together?

Available Now

BROKEN PIECES

Can three broken pieces make a whole?

Josiah Evans is the orphan who lost both his parents. He's sweet, shy, and all heart. He wants nothing more than to be loved.

Mateo Sanchez is the son of a gang leader. He's seen it all, and never hesitates to do what needs to be done, no matter what it is.

Tristan Croft is the wealthy attorney who clawed his way up from the bottom to rule his own world. He'll never depend on anyone but himself again.

Three men who couldn't be more different…and yet, as their lives intersect, they find an uncommon balance that calms the storms inside each of them, and ignites fires hotter than they ever thought imaginable.

Told in three parts and spanning over ten years, BROKEN PIECES is a journey of healing for three fragmented souls, finding love in the unlikeliest of places—with each other.

ABOUT THE AUTHOR:

Riley Hart is the girl who wears her heart on her sleeve. She's a hopeless romantic. A lover of sexy stories, passionate men, and writing about all the trouble they can get into together. If she's not writing, you'll probably find her reading.

Riley lives in California with her awesome family, who she is thankful for every day.

You can find her online at:

Twitter

@RileyHart5

Facebook

https://www.facebook.com/riley.hart.1238?fref=ts

Blog

www.rileyhartwrites.blogspot.com

Tumblr

http://rileyhartwrites.tumblr.com

STAY

Made in the USA
San Bernardino, CA
30 January 2015